The Cat That Could
Spell Mississippi

The Cat That Could Spell Mississippi

LAURA HAWKINS

Houghton Mifflin Company
Boston 1992

Library of Congress Cataloging-in-Publication Data

Hawkins, Laura.
  The cat that could spell Mississippi / Laura Hawkins.
    p. cm.
  Summary: Anxious to prove that she is special at her new school,
fourth-grader Linda makes everything more difficult for herself when
she cheats on a spelling bee.
  ISBN 0-395-61627-1
  [1. Honesty — Fiction. 2. Schools — Fiction. 3. Cats — Fiction.
4. Friendship — Fiction. 5. Moving, Household — Fiction.] I. Title.
PZ7.H313517Cat 1992   92-8025
                              CIP
                              AC
[Fic] — dc20

Printed in the United States of America

AGM 10 9 8 7 6 5 4 3 2 1

With love to Dad —
my "people watcher" mentor

The Cat That Could Spell Mississippi

1

When Mrs. Crandall introduced Linda Cappanelli to the fourth-grade class, no one in the room said a word.

Not "howdy" like when Linda had lived in Texas. Not "yo" like in St. Louis; not even a New York City "Hey, you!"

Finally, Eddie Wilcox blurted out, "We don't need any more girls in this class!"

Tammy Collins smirked at Eddie. Then she told Linda, "We need boys. All we have now is animals."

Eddie scowled at Tammy. Tammy smirked back. Then Eddie said, "Takes an animal to know an animal."

Linda figured Eddie was right about that. She hadn't been in the room ten minutes and already she felt about as welcome as a skunk. Being accepted at Riverview Elementary was going to be some trick.

"I have a cat," Linda said. Then, because she desperately needed to catch the attention of the class, she made something up. "He can spell his own name. Mississippi."

Linda said that because Mississippi was the hardest word she could spell.

Tammy rolled her eyes at Linda. "We don't care about your dumb old spelling cat. We want to know if *you* can spell."

"Children, children!" Mrs. Crandall clapped her hands. Her green eyes narrowed at Eddie and Tammy. They softened when they looked at Linda.

"Since you haven't been with us these first two months of school, Linda," Mrs. Crandall said, still eyeing Eddie and Tammy, "you wouldn't know that we are having a spelling contest. Boys against the girls. Whichever team has the best percentage of weekly words spelled correctly will choose a speller to represent our class in the all-school spelling bee."

Linda nodded. Now she understood. She understood, too, that to be accepted by the girls in the class, she was going to have to be a good speller. But she wasn't a good speller!

"My mom and dad were in a contest once. In

San Francisco," Linda offered. "They're magicians. Cappanelli The Great. They made my brother, Ian, disappear."

Eddie Wilcox called from the back of the room, "How about if *you* disappear?"

"That's enough, Eddie," Mrs. Crandall said curtly. She turned to Linda. "When would you like to try taking this week's spelling test, Linda? You can take it on Monday if you like. Since you haven't had time to study the words, no one can expect you to do well on a test you haven't studied." Her green eyes pointedly swept around the class.

Linda knew just what to say to impress the class. "I'd like to try taking the test today."

She was right — as if by magic, every head in the class turned towards her as if she'd said something really important.

Mrs. Crandall smiled and handed Linda a speller with a list of words for her to study.

Linda didn't study the words. Instead, during math time, she copied the list of words from the speller Mrs. Crandall gave her. The list was so small that it fit nicely inside the long sleeve of her new white blouse, which her mother had sent her in the mail from Tallahassee.

During the spelling test, every time Mrs. Crandall called out a word, Linda sneaked a peek at her list to spell the word correctly.

She was the only one in the whole class who spelled every word right!

At recess, three girls came over to where Linda was standing. Linda remembered their names from class. They were Tammy Collins, Libby Grimes and Jill Kramer.

"How come you got a perfect paper today?" Tammy asked. "I bet it was luck," she grumbled. "Beginner's luck. I bet you couldn't do it again."

"Sure she could," Jill argued. "She used magic, just like her parents, didn't you, Linda?"

"Anyone who can spell that good without even studying is sure to win the spelling bee," Libby reasoned.

"But how do we know it isn't a fluke?" Tammy insisted. "Do something else with magic," she challenged Linda.

Linda picked up an abandoned basketball nearby. She tossed the ball up in the air and spun it like her father had shown her, balancing it on her finger.

"See. What did I tell you!" Jill squealed, watching the ball twirl.

"That's not magic," Tammy grumbled.

Jill ignored Tammy. Instead, she looked at Linda. "The class that wins the spelling bee gets a special party." Her eyes widened with anticipation.

Linda was excited, too, because Jill was starting to like her!

But then she began to worry. She hadn't spelled the words on her own. But Jill didn't have to know that, did she? Just like her father's audiences didn't know about hidden trap doors and secret compartments. Except now Jill wanted Linda to win her a party. Would her new friends keep wanting things from her that she couldn't get without cheating?

Jill jumped up and down. "I know! Let's go somewhere special after school and make party plans for when Linda wins the spelling bee."

"Can you go with us after school?" Libby asked Linda.

"Of course she can," Tammy said, speaking for Linda. "And I know just the place to go."

Linda studied Tammy's sneaky look. She didn't trust Tammy.

"Grams wouldn't know where I am," Linda said, hesitating. "I live with my grandmother and grandfather while my parents are gone on the road. Grams is very strict."

But Tammy had made up her mind. "You won't

get in trouble when you get home," she sniffed. "But if you do, you can use magic to get out of it. Right?" she said, challenging Linda.

Linda thought of Grams, pacing the floor, wondering why Linda hadn't come straight home from school. But then she glanced at Jill, who was wide-eyed and expectant. She didn't want to lose Jill as a friend.

"Wel-l, sure," she said slowly. "I suppose I can use magic." A twinkle glinted in her eye. "I'll tell Grams I made my new friends disappear and had trouble getting them back."

Tammy exchanged a wary look with Libby, and then left Linda alone for a while.

But cheating on the spelling test still bothered Linda. It stalked her like a hungry beast.

2

"Pizza, pizza, pizza," Tammy whined. "I want a pizza party."

If Tammy wanted pizza so much, Linda wondered, why then had she insisted that the four girls come to this tiny diner after school?

There was no pizza on the menu, and the diner itself didn't seem like the type of place Tammy would choose. The floor linoleum was cracked and worn. The red vinyl covering the booths had been patched with gray duct tape. Even the waitress sagged as she cleared the neighboring booth of faded coffee cups.

"Mrs. Crandall said we can have any kind of party we want if our class wins the spelling bee," Jill reminded them. "Maybe we could even have a skating party!"

"Yeah, but our class has to win the spelling bee first," Libby pointed out.

"We'll win, won't we, Linda?" Tammy asked. She stared at Linda with a look that made Linda nervous.

"Well, I don't know." Linda fidgeted in her seat. "I mean, nobody knows. I can't know what words will be asked. So how can I know if I can spell them?"

"Magic!" Jill exclaimed, clapping her hands.

Tammy glanced around at her companions with a secretive look. "I have a plan to find out if Linda is the one who should be in the spelling bee."

"Of course she's the one. None of the rest of us can spell as good," Jill said, looking puzzled.

Tammy wore a satisfied smile. "We have to find out for sure," she said. And when the waitress came to take their order, Tammy asked the woman, "You're Parmalee Swain, aren't you?"

"In the flesh," Parmalee said, which caused the girls to notice that Parmalee had a lot of "flesh" to be in. "And who we got here?"

Tammy introduced herself and each of her companions. "We've come for you to tell our fortunes."

A hush fell over the table.

Parmalee threaded her pencil into her brassy red hair above her ear. Her hazel-flecked blue eyes studied the four of them. "Did my sister send you?

Did Bernadette Weisen put you up to this? Well, you've come to the wrong place. I don't tell fortunes! My sister tells fortunes. After our big split, we made an agreement. She got the house. I got the diner. She don't cook no food. I don't tell no fortunes. You can tell Bernadette that her trying to trick me like this won't make me speak to her. But here's a prediction for Bernadette. Tell her that cats will start spelling their names before I speak to her again!"

Tammy looked at Libby. Libby looked at Jill. All three of them looked at Linda.

Linda gulped. She'd made that up about her cat being able to spell its name!

"Linda has a cat that can spell its name!" Jill blurted out.

Libby poked Jill to make her be quiet. Her face widened. "We don't even know your sister," Libby said.

Tammy's chin jutted out. "My aunt Caroline said she came in here only a week ago and you told her she was going to meet an interesting man. And she did!"

"Well, if I did tell her that, I wasn't holding it out to be gospel. It was a coincidence, that's all. Now what you going to order?"

9

"We don't want anything to eat. Aunt Caroline said the food here is terrible."

Parmalee snorted. "So who is your aunt Caroline? Some relation to Sara Lee?"

Tammy's face clouded. "She's my mother's younger sister."

Parmalee threw up her hands. "Didn't I just tell you that sisters are trouble? That's why I haven't spoken to mine in a whole year. But if you want fortunes, you go speak to *her*."

"My Aunt Caroline said you were real. What you told her about meeting a tall handsome stranger came true!" Tammy took out a limp dollar bill. The other three girls glanced at each other. Considering Parmalee's attitude, a dollar bill was not going to buy much of a fortune.

"We don't need a big fortune told. We need to know if Linda Cappanelli, here, is going to win our school spelling bee."

"Well, that's a pretty big fortune if you ask me," Parmalee said. "There'll be seven other spellers in that bee."

"Wow, how did you know that?" Jill asked.

"I know lots of things. I know you girls are students of Mrs. Crandall."

"You could have guessed that," Libby Grimes reasoned.

"I could have. But I didn't."

Linda shifted uncomfortably in her seat. Until now, she didn't believe in fortunetellers. Fortune-tellers were like magicians. She knew the magic her mom and dad performed was all tricks. She hadn't believed Parmalee was a fortuneteller because Parmalee said she wasn't. But now Parmalee was saying things that were true, and she couldn't risk Parmalee telling her fortune — she couldn't risk Parmalee saying she had cheated on the spelling test.

"I don't want my fortune told."

The three other girls stared at Linda.

"Why not?" Tammy asked.

"I don't want to know things before they happen." Linda hoped that would make Tammy drop the fortunetelling idea.

"But you knew you were going to do well on the spelling test today. Otherwise, you wouldn't have taken the test without studying. That's knowing things before they happen."

Linda wished Libby would keep quiet.

"We have to know so we can plan for our party!" Jill piped up. "If you aren't going to win, Linda, what's the use in planning anything?"

"I think you're just being stubborn," Tammy said, "because Parmalee can do better magic than you. If you don't want your fortune told, I'm leaving."

"Me too." Libby stood up with Tammy.

"Sure you don't want to spend that dollar first?" Parmalee asked. "I got some fresh pumpkin pie I could let go for a quarter a piece."

But she was too late. Tammy and Libby were already out the door, taking the dollar with them.

"Gee, Linda, I don't know what harm a little fortune would do you," Jill said, reluctantly standing up. "Couldn't you go along with it? Fortune-telling is just as much fun as magic. And Parmalee would have said you were going to win the spelling bee, wouldn't you have, Parmalee? Fortune-tellers always say what people want to hear."

And sometimes they said things that were too close to the truth! Linda thought.

"Well, now, I never told the fortune so I'm not saying what I would have said." Parmalee moved on to another booth and began collecting dirty cups.

"See? She doesn't know," Linda pointed out to Jill.

"Of course she does," Jill argued. "Maybe it's *you* who's been faking *your* magic." Then Jill shuffled out the door to join Tammy and Libby.

Linda's stunned gaze caught Parmalee's curious glance. Linda looked down. She didn't want Parmalee to see the tears forming in her eyes. She didn't want anyone to know that she might be the very first person in Riverview to gain and lose three friends all in the same day.

The next thing Linda knew, Parmalee was standing over the booth again with a piece of pumpkin pie. She set the pie down in front of Linda. "No charge," she said, and slumped down in the seat opposite Linda.

Linda didn't really want the pie, but she did want a friend. She picked up the fork and tasted the pie out of politeness. It tasted like boiled tennis shoes!

"You cheated today on the test," Parmalee said.

Linda dropped her fork. "You know I cheated?"

"As sure as it's written all over your face."

Linda glanced at the window that flanked the booth in search of her reflection. If something like that was written all over her face, she wanted to see it!

"I don't see anything!"

Parmalee laughed. "No, honey, that's an expression. It means, I know by the way you're acting."

"You do?"

13

Parmalee nodded. "What I can't figure out is why a smart girl like you would do something like that."

Linda glanced down at the pie in front of her. What *she* couldn't figure out was why Parmalee's pie tasted so awful! If Parmalee sold food for a living, she should know how to make it good, shouldn't she?

"It was magic," Linda explained about the spelling test. "Can I help it if my parents are magicians and they taught me how to make things that I want happen?"

Parmalee swayed back in her seat. "You wanted to cheat on the spelling test?"

Linda glanced down. No, she hadn't wanted to cheat. But she couldn't figure any other way to make friends.

"Do you like serving bad food?" she asked, avoiding Parmalee's question about cheating.

Parmalee cast Linda a steely look.

"I know somebody who can cook really good," Linda said quickly, thinking of her grandmother, hoping to soften what she had said about Parmalee's cooking. She wanted to help Parmalee instead of criticize her.

"So do I," Parmalee said. "My sister, Bernadette." A wounded look surfaced on Parmalee's face. "But then this place would have to be called 'Bernadette's Diner' instead of 'Parmalee's.' At least that's what Bernadette told me when we had our big fight and split up." She shrugged. "I've always had a fondness for my name in lights. My name on a marquee."

"Yeah," Linda said, just as dreamily. "I'd sure like to win the school spelling bee. And a medal with my name on it. That would show everybody in my class once and for all."

"What would it show them?" Parmalee asked.

Linda stopped to think about that. What *would* winning the spelling bee show them? "It'd show them that there's something special about me."

"I declare," Parmalee said, making her voice rise up so it sounded really surprised. "They already know there's something special about you. They just don't know what it is."

"Do *you* know what it is, Parmalee?"

Parmalee made a *kahumm* noise in her throat. "I know what isn't special about you. That cheating business. That kind of thing turns a silk purse into a sow's ear."

Linda looked down at the terrible-tasting pie in front of her. To look at its golden color, a person

15

would have thought that pie might be good enough to win a blue ribbon. But it was bitter to the taste.

She glanced sideways at the window again, half expecting to catch a glimpse of herself as a big pig ear. But like the pie, she was the same as before on the outside. Anyway, it was her insides she wanted to see the most. She couldn't, though — she could only feel them.

That's when she suddenly had a great urge to oink!

3

Two blocks short of Grams and Grampy's house, Linda spotted Ian walking. His dark brown curls flopped down over his bent head, and he kicked rocks from the path. His right arm was folded against his chest. There was a sling holding it in place!

"Ian, what happened!" Linda ran hard to catch up with her brother.

"You told." Ian glared at Linda, still kicking rocks. "You told about Mom and Dad being magicians. Didn't I tell you not to tell? Everybody at basketball practice knew. Cory Richards told everybody. He said our whole family was cheats."

Linda gulped. "Is that how you got your arm hurt?"

"I couldn't let him get away with that, could I?"

"You got in a fight?"

Ian nodded. "Now I can't even play basketball

17

at all. Coach says he thinks it's a sprained wrist. It should get better in a week or two." He kicked hard at the sidewalk. "But by then, everybody else will be ahead of me. They'll be better."

"I'm sorry, Ian," Linda said, trying to comfort him. "You'll catch up. And when your arm is better, you'll still get to play, won't you?"

Ian shook his head. "Coach says Cory and me would have to patch up our differences before either of us get to play. But I'm not patching up differences with anybody who called me a cheat." Ian pointed a finger at Linda. "Just don't tell Grampy. Grampy was the one that convinced Mom and Dad to let us come live a whole school year in one place."

Linda noticed that Ian didn't say anything about Grampy and basketball. It was Grampy who had urged Ian to play. Ian was a terrible basketball player, and Linda suspected that he played because he didn't want to disappoint Grampy.

Linda bounded onto the Cappanelli front porch and opened the storm door for Ian, fishing a hand into the mailbox hanging next to the door. "Look, Ian, letters!" She sorted out two identical envelopes from the rest of the mail. One was addressed to her and the other to Ian. Linda knew they were from their parents, who were presently performing in Florida. "You want me to open yours for you?"

"Naw. I'll look at it later." With his left hand, Ian stashed his envelope in his jacket pocket and pushed through the door.

"Heaven have mercy!" Grams cried. "Ian Cappanelli, what has that horrid basketball done to you?"

Grams swooshed over and inspected Ian's arm. Grams was good at swooshing. Mostly Grams was good at swooshing Grampy. Right now Grampy was pretty spry himself. He popped out of his easy chair and sprang over to Ian to have a look at the arm. His eyes bugged out of his broad face. "I was afraid this might happen if I didn't come to practice today."

Ian rubbed his hurt wrist. "Coach says a sprain."

"Well, we're marching to the hospital right now and getting that wrist x-rayed," Grams announced. She snatched her jacket from the closet and guided Ian towards the back door.

"If you'll hang on a minute, Linda and I are coming, too." Grampy waddled to the closet.

"No, you're not. You've had your turn filling the boy's head with basketball. You stay here and

19

finish supper. Don't let the spaghetti sauce scorch. And don't you two snack on those cookies you've got hidden somewhere. You better be good and hungry when we get back."

"Nag, nag, nag," Grampy said, slumping back down in his chair. But he said it only after he knew Grams was out the door and couldn't hear him.

"Look, Grampy," Linda said, showing him her letter. She opened the envelope and two dollars floated to the floor.

"Well, Lin Lin, what are you going to do now that you're rich?"

Linda knew exactly what she was going to do with the money. "I'm going to have my fortune told."

"Fortune told?" He smiled. "I can tell you your fortune right here and now for nothing. You're going to grow up beautiful and twice as smart. And you'll never nag your husband about his pot belly or his hankering for sweets or his smoking cigars out back of the garage."

"Oh, Grampy," Linda said. "That's how *you* want me to grow up. What if I turn out to be a nag? Will you still love me?"

"I love your grandma, don't I?"

Linda laughed and kissed Grampy on his bald

forehead, right between his two patches of silver hair, on the place where he said Grams had scalped him when she'd caught him licking the icing off one of her Tropical Sunshine cakes.

"Want a cookie?" Grampy asked.

"Grampy! You know you can't have a cookie. It's bad for your sugar level." Linda pretended to swat him on his hand.

"Now you're scaring me, Lin Lin girl. You're sounding just like your grandma. And speaking of her, I'd better stir the spaghetti sauce before it scorches."

He heaved himself up and waddled to the kitchen. With a big fanfare, he whooshed off the lid of the big kettle of simmering red sauce and began poking at it with a long wooden spoon.

"Grampy," Linda began, watching him. "Do you ever cheat?"

Grampy stood still a moment. Then he began to pick little yellow specks out of the sauce and deposit them onto a dish on the counter at the side of the stove. "Yes, Lin Lin, I suppose I do. Your grandmother likes garlic in her sauce, but I don't. If I pick out half of what she put in here, she'll never know. Guess that would be cheating in your grandmother's book."

"Grams says garlic is good for your circulation,"

21

Linda reminded him. "But I don't mean that kind of cheating. I mean some other kind of cheating. Promise you won't tell Ian I told you?"

"Promise." Grampy hooked his little finger around Linda's little finger, their own secret sign that they had an agreement.

Then Linda told Grampy what Ian had told her about Cory Richards and how Cory had said Ian was a cheat. "Why do you think he said that?"

Grampy stopped picking garlic from the sauce. An odd look came over his face, then he made a gurgling noise as he cleared his throat. Linda sensed he felt uncomfortable and didn't want to answer her. Could Cory Richards have told the truth?

"Oh, that's just talk," Grampy finally said. "What better way for Cory Richards to make Ian lose his head than to call him a cheat?"

"Yeah, what better way," Linda repeated, wanting to believe Grampy. She also wanted to distance herself from him and let him find his old self before they talked more. "Think I'll take a walk."

"A cat walk?" Grampy asked before Linda could slip on her jacket and sneak out the back door.

"Oh, Grampy," Linda moaned. "I wish you weren't so good at reading my mind."

"And I wish you would leave that stray cat alone. That animal is wild. No way to tame it. Even if you do get close to it, it might scratch your eyes out. You think I want a blind granddaughter?"

Yes, Linda thought, Grampy did want a blind granddaughter when it came to certain subjects. Like cheating.

"Okay, so maybe I'll go hunting for your cookies instead," Linda said, causing Grampy to smile.

Grampy always had a package or two of cookies stashed in the garage, hidden from Grams. Whenever he got a craving for sugar, he would make an excuse to clean the car or decide to work with his power tools. Linda knew of at least two of his favorite hiding places: under the table-saw cabinet and above the garage-door opener.

"If I didn't have this sauce to stir, I'd come with you," Grampy assured her. "How's about you bring me a couple of double-fudge sandwiches?

"It's a deal."

Linda bounced out the back door and ran at full speed to the single garage at the end of the yard. Entering it, she spotted Ian's basketball on the special holder Grampy had built for him. She took it down and twirled it on her finger, as she had done at school. Then she stepped outside and shot a few baskets at the hoop Grampy had hung over the garage door especially for Ian. Both shots swished the net. That's when she heard something inside the garage. It was a cat's meow.

Ball in hand, she stepped slowly and softly back inside the garage, calling in a soothing tone of voice, "Kitty? Here, kitty kitty."

When there was no answer, Linda stepped to the table saw to check for cookies. But then she heard it!

No. It couldn't be! But, yes! She had actually heard it!

It was a cat's meow, all right, but it sounded different. It sounded like the cat meowed and hissed and sputtered. It sounded like the cat had spelled Mississippi!

The sound came from an old tire hanging high up on the wall. Mississippi was using the old tire for a place to perch. The gray cat lay curled along the tire's bottom curve, yellow eyes starkly visible against the drab background.

Linda quivered with fright. What did it mean, the cat spelling Mississippi like Linda had said, like Parmalee had also predicted?

Linda didn't know. It could be a coincidence,

she decided. Like the fortune Parmalee had told for Tammy Collins's aunt that came true. Or it might mean that Mississippi was the clue to something very important Linda didn't understand. All she knew was that she still wanted to befriend the cat. Maybe it could spell other words. Maybe it could spell out a message to her!

" 'Sippi? Want a cookie?" Linda slowly retrieved the package of double-fudge sandwich cookies from under the table saw, but the crackling sound of her tearing open the cellophane caused Mississippi to fly out of the tire to the ground and scramble out the door.

Linda ran after the cat, several cookies still in her hand. " 'Sippi, 'Sippi, don't run away. I've got something for you."

The cat dashed across the alley and into the neighbor's yard. Linda followed him. Mississippi loped up onto the wraparound porch of the paint-cracked white house. A breeze stirred the sign hanging on chains from a post near the porch steps. When the chains creaked, the sound scared Mississippi. He flew off the porch and disappeared.

Linda stepped closer to the sign in order to read it. The sign had a startling big eye at the top, which seemed to watch out over the whole yard.

Below the eye on the sign was written "Madame Weisen, Your Future Revealed."

Linda was sure that Mississippi had brought her to Parmalee's sister's house on purpose. But like the cat, when the wind swayed the chains on the sign and it moaned eerily, she scrambled away and ran home.

4

On Thursday morning at school, Linda spotted Jill near the water fountain. She flashed the two dollars that her parents had sent her so Jill could see the money.

"We can go to Parmalee's sister's after school today to have my fortune told." Linda didn't want to go alone.

Jill eyed Linda skeptically. "Parmalee is the real fortuneteller. Everybody in town knows that."

"But Parmalee told us to go to her sister's."

"I'd never go there," Jill said, her eyes widening. "That place is spooky."

"But that's the way fortunetellers are supposed to be," Linda argued.

"I don't care," Jill said. "I'm never going there." She walked away to join the others.

Linda stuffed the two dollars back in her pocket. She had been afraid of this — that Jill wouldn't agree to go with her. Why should she? She already had friends. And if those friends didn't believe in Linda's magic anymore, then Jill didn't either.

Linda should have told Jill about Mississippi. She should have invited Jill to Grampy's garage to hear the cat spell his name — then she could have told Jill how Mississippi led her to Bernadette's house. It wasn't Linda's idea to go to Bernadette's house to have her fortune told; it was Mississippi's. And since Jill would think Mississippi was a magical cat, she would understand why Linda had to go there!

But now, Linda's only hope was the letter she'd received from her parents — in the letter, her parents had promised a wonderful surprise. The Cappanellis were coming home to Grams and Grampy's for Thanksgiving, only three weeks away! Maybe, just maybe, Linda could ask her parents to put on a free show for her classmates! Everybody in class would want to be friends with her then, whether she was a good speller or not.

Linda would have to plan breaking her news very carefully. She wouldn't tell Libby. Libby was the kind of person who might not like magic shows. She was always trying to figure things out. With magic, a person had to believe. It ruined the fun to try to figure out how a trick is done.

She was also afraid to tell Tammy. Tammy would be impressed that Linda could get her parents to perform for the class, but it would make her angry that they were Linda's parents. Linda, the person who got a perfect paper on her first spelling test. It would be too much!

No, it had to be Jill. Jill loved surprises, and she would not try to figure out why Linda wanted her parents to perform for the class. She would be excited about magicians coming to school. Her party plans would be complete!

Linda waited until the first recess to try to speak to Jill alone. That was pretty hard, though, because Mrs. Crandall dropped a big bomb on the class before they filed out for recess — she announced that the spelling test on next Wednesday would contain some of all the words the class had had during the previous nine weeks. A midterm review, she called it. Everybody groaned.

Linda scrambled to be one of the first out the door for recess. Jill was the first.

"Hey, Jill, wait up."

Jill stopped and swung around to face Linda.

"I have an idea for a class party," Linda blurted out. Then she told about her parents. She didn't realize that Tammy was standing behind her until she was through explaining that her magician parents were coming to Riverview for Thanksgiving.

"How do we know you even have magician parents?" Tammy challenged her.

Jill hadn't even had a chance to open her mouth!

"I think you made that up about magician parents," Tammy continued. "Why don't you go play with Marcella Starbuckle? She's the class liar. You two should have fun together making things up."

Linda didn't move an inch, even though Tammy had scared her. "I'm not lying. Come to my grandparents' house after school. They have a poster with my parents' picture on it."

"We have plans after school," Tammy said, sniffing and half closing her eyes.

"We're starting a new club," Jill blurted out.

"And you're not invited," Tammy said, guiding Jill away from Linda.

Linda watched as the two of them bounced away, giggling. How could she have messed things up so badly?

At lunch, Linda sat alone in the cafeteria. She didn't even go out to recess in the afternoon. She stayed in the classroom and looked at the eight lists of spelling words the class had taken in the weeks before she arrived.

It was obvious to Linda that she couldn't cheat

on the spelling test on Wednesday. She couldn't stuff nine lists of spelling words up her blouse sleeve! And even if she could, Mrs. Crandall was going to mix the words up, taking words from all the lists, only which ones?

After school, Linda hugged her speller to her chest and ran to Parmalee's Diner.

"I'm a sow's ear, all right," she told the heavyset waitress. "There's nothing special about me. I can't do anything better than anybody else."

"In that case, you can have anything on the menu for free," Parmalee said.

"Why?"

"Because with you eating my food, I won't have to listen to you say how much better you can cook than me. Can I interest you in a slice of coconut cream pie?"

Linda shook her head.

"Tell you what. I got some extra rich brownies with peanut butter icing."

Reluctantly, Linda nodded her head. Parmalee brought the brownie for Linda and a slice of pie for herself. She sighed as she sank down opposite Linda. She sighed again after Linda had told her everything that had happened to her since leaving Parmalee the day before.

Linda tried a nibble of Parmalee's brownie. It tasted like liver. Yuck. She hated liver. She pushed the plate away from her. "Is tasting one of your brownies what it takes to be your friend?"

"Bad batch, huh?" Parmalee shrugged. "Oh, well. Friends take you for what you are."

"Then you don't mind if I'm a nobody?" Linda asked.

"I wouldn't if you were. But you aren't."

"How am I a somebody, Parmalee?" Linda asked.

"You're my friend, aren't you? That makes you a somebody."

Linda nodded. But it wasn't enough. Parmalee seemed to sense this. She nudged at the last bit of meringue with her fork. Then she said, "Figure out what's special about you. Not your parents. Not your grandparents. Not your brother. But you."

Linda sighed. So far, the only thing she was good at was not eating Parmalee's food. And judging from the fact there were no other customers in the diner, that was a specialty of everybody in town.

5

All the way home from Parmalee's, Linda tried to think of something that was special about her. She couldn't think of anything.

She wasn't good at performing in front of people like her parents. She wasn't good at making things perfect like Grams.

The person whom she was most like was Grampy, she supposed. She tried to think of what Grampy was good at to see if she was good at the same thing. He probably had been good at lots of things when he was younger, she figured, but now that he was old and retired, all she could think of that he was good at was hiding cookies in the garage. He was especially good at that!

This made Linda think about how she had been good at cheating on the spelling test. But she didn't *feel* good about cheating — there had to be something else!

Trudging up the alley in back of Grams and

Grampy's house, Linda decided that she must be good at seeing things. Somehow, Parmalee had magically been transported from her diner to the neighbor's back yard! Only now, instead of a waitress uniform, she wore gardening clothes and a brown sock top over her red curls.

She was digging with a shovel in what had once been a flourishing garden. After several hard freezes, it was now cluttered with sagging foliage the color of tea leaves.

Linda had been thinking that, since she couldn't think of anything special about herself, she needed for someone else to tell her. She realized she was now looking at Bernadette, Parmalee's sister, the fortuneteller! Who better to help her find herself than Bernadette?

"Hi, Bernadette," she called, walking over to the woman. "What are you doing?"

Bernadette glanced up from where she was, bent over on hands and knees pulling carrots out of the ground. Her face was flushed with pink and her eyes were watery from the crisp November air. She looked exactly like Parmalee, only thinner. They were twins!

She didn't sound like Parmalee. "Hello, little girl."

34

"My name is Linda."

"Well, Linda, I'm pretty busy right now. I can't talk." She stood up and scooped her pile of pale carrots into a big crock bowl. Then she bent over and lifted the bowl to her chest, stumbling off towards her house.

"Are you feeling all right, Bernadette?" Linda didn't know Bernadette at all but, since she did know Parmalee and that the two didn't act alike, she sensed that something was wrong. Bernadette held onto that bowl of carrots in a strangely protective way.

"I really can't talk right now."

Linda reached into her pocket and fished out the two dollars her parents had sent her. She ran to catch up with Bernadette and show her the money. "Can you tell my fortune? Your sister, Parmalee Swain, said you tell fortunes." Linda held out the money. "I can pay you."

Bernadette stopped midway up her porch steps. She looked at the money and then at Linda and then back at the money. "My sister sent you?"

Linda nodded.

Bernadette cast Linda a look of disbelief. Finally she said, "How *is* Parmalee?"

"She's very smart." Because her answer sounded

funny, she added, "She's still serving bad food." Being a fortuneteller, Bernadette ought to know more about Parmalee than Linda should, especially since she was her own sister, oughtn't she?

Bernadette laughed. But it wasn't the same throaty laugh as Parmalee's. It was more quiet and mysterious.

"You mean she's giving away food, don't you?"

"Along with free advice," Linda said.

Bernadette shrugged and motioned for Linda to follow her inside. Bernadette's house had a strange feel to it. Only one light was lit in the dining room, which made the rest of the house seem cold and lonely. Maybe that was why Bernadette didn't take off her coat. She crooked a finger at Linda for her to follow her to the kitchen. It was a finger much skinnier than Parmalee's.

Linda watched as Bernadette dumped the carrots into the sink and ran water over them. Then she watched as Bernadette opened a lower cupboard and pulled out a big pan. When Bernadette opened the refrigerator to take out a container, Linda stifled a gasp. There was no food in that refrigerator! There were a few jars of pickles and mustard and ketchup, but most of the space was empty.

"Something else you needed?" Bernadette asked Linda.

Linda was still stunned by the empty refrigerator. It took her a few moments to think of something to say. "My fortune. You were going to tell my fortune."

Bernadette poured the container of broth into the pan and added water to it. Then she peeled the carrots into the trash can. "Your fortune. Hmm. Let's see. What did you say your name was again?"

"Linda."

"Yes. Linda. And you live ..."

"I live across the alley from you. With my grandparents and my brother." Gee, did Linda have to draw fortuneteller Bernadette a diagram?

"Yes. And you want to know what you'll be when you grow up. Right?"

"No. I already know what I'm going to be when I grow up. I'm going to be like my grandfather."

"Oh."

"I want to know if I'm going to get any better at spelling. I want to know if I'm going to win the Riverview Elementary spelling bee."

"Why, of course you are. You're like your grandfather, aren't you?"

"No. Grams was the one good at spelling when

37

she was my age. I don't know what Grampy was good at when he was my age."

"Well, then, don't you think you'd better ask him?"

Linda stopped to think about that a minute. It *did* make sense. She *would* ask Grampy. But the thing she couldn't figure out was why she was asking Bernadette. Bernadette was no good as a fortuneteller — Linda was the one who had to tell things to her. Still, the conversation wasn't all for nothing, as Linda smelled something good coming from the pot on Bernadette's stove. It smelled better than something Grams might make.

"What is that?" Linda pointed at the pot.

"Soup. Want to try?"

Bernadette scooped up a spoonful and guided it into Linda's mouth. Yum. The soup was delicious! But there wasn't enough for two, Linda judged, glancing at the pot. There probably wasn't even enough for Bernadette. Maybe that was why she was so skinny.

The soup was so good that it made Linda hungry; she was ready to go home and get something to eat. She raced out of the house and across Bernadette's yard to Grampy's garage.

Mississippi wasn't in the garage. Grampy must

have been successful at keeping him out, although he suspected the cat had a secret entry into the garage that he hadn't discovered and plugged up.

Linda got the stepladder and unfolded it underneath the garage-door opener. She found a package of cookies lying directly on top of the opener. Scotch shortbread.

She looked at the cookies and then thought of Bernadette's delicious but meager soup and the refrigerator with no food in it. She ran back to Bernadette's house with the cookies, sneaking them into the dining room, laying them on the table, a nice surprise for Bernadette after she ate her soup. Under the cookies, she placed her two dollars.

6

Mississippi was in the garage when Linda returned. He hissed and sputtered his name. Instead of perching on the old tire, he sat on Ian's basketball holder. He had never done that before, and Linda wondered what it might mean.

She found one of the few remaining double-fudge sandwich cookies in the table-saw cabinet. This time she crumbled it into little pieces in her hand so Mississippi could not grab a big piece and run away from her.

Linda extended her hand to Mississippi, trying to coax the cat to come get the cookie. Mississippi jumped off of the basketball rack onto the roof of Grampy's car. Then he eased down the windshield to Linda's hand. He creeped slowly toward Linda and then gorged the cookie pieces while Linda slowly eased her other hand up to the cat's shoulder and stroked the fluffy fur. Once.

Cookie eaten, Mississippi retreated with one swift bound back to the roof of Grampy's car, hunkered down, curled his tail around his side, and sat watching Linda.

That's when Linda heard the *ping, ping, ping* of Ian's basketball hit the cement outside behind the garage. Mississippi jerked into an upright position and flew to his normal tire perch, his yellow eyes lit with fright.

Why did Ian have to scare Mississippi? Linda thought, sighing. She might have gotten the cat to come back to her again. Well, at least Mississippi had not run completely away after she gave him the cookie — she was making progress taming the cat. But she knew she might as well give up with Ian around.

She stepped outside the garage to the cement slab. "I thought you couldn't practice," Linda said to Ian, watching her brother, who was dribbling the ball with his left instead of right hand. He no longer wore the sling, but Linda could tell he tried not to use his sore wrist any more than he had to.

"Shh. Don't tell Grams. I'm not supposed to be doing this, but I can't let all the others get ahead of me."

Ian swatted the ball against the cement, caught

41

its bounce, brought it to his chest, and flung it at the metal hoop above the garage door. The ball dangled for a moment on the rim and then fell away from the basket.

Linda groaned.

"Hope you're satisfied, Cory Richards." Ian slapped the ball against the cement and then proceeded to do the whole thing over, missing the basket again.

"Is he still bothering you?" Linda asked. "Cory Richards?"

Ian rolled his dark eyes.

"Is he still calling you a cheat?"

Ian shrugged. "Well," he said, hesitating. "Not exactly a cheat."

"Then what?"

Ian dribbled the ball a couple of times. "Now he's calling me a hog." He aimed the ball again and shot, missing.

"Never you mind about Cory Richards," Grampy's booming voice echoed. He waddled out the back door of the garage. "You just keep your mind on the game." He glanced over at Linda and crooked a finger at her. "You and me need to have a talk."

Linda shuffled reluctantly toward Grampy,

meekly following him inside the garage. She knew what was coming. Grampy missed his cookies. But once he found out what she'd done with them, he wouldn't really mind, would he?

"Now I'm a sharing person, Lin Lin. But there's a limit to my charity." He pointed up to the garage-door opener. "I just scared that cat out of here, and it was looking a might more plump than usual. You have anything to say about my missing cookies?"

"It wasn't Mississippi, Grampy." Linda glanced down at the floor. *"I* took that package of cookies."

"You ate 'em?"

Linda shook her head. "I gave them away."

Grampy sighed. "Hmm. Who'd you give them to?"

Linda pointed in the direction of Bernadette's house. "The lady that lives over there. She didn't have one single thing in her refrigerator. I think she's having carrots for supper — carrots she got out of her garden that weren't very good ones."

Grampy rubbed the back of his neck, looking as if he didn't quite know how to handle the situation.

"That lady can get a real job anytime she wants and buy her own cookies. Fortuneteller.

Hummph! I'm not sure you're helping by giving her cookies."

"I gave her my two dollars, too."

"Your two dollars?" That really confused Grampy.

"For telling my fortune. Only she didn't do a very good job," Linda explained. "I had to tell her most of the stuff about me myself. She told me I was going to grow up to be just like you. So if I want to know what I'm going to be good at, I'm supposed to ask *you*. I guess I already know what I'm good at. I'm good at hiding and finding cookies."

"And giving them away," Grampy reminded her. "And feeding them to stray cats." He playfully pinched her nose. "No, Lin Lin, you don't take after me. You take after Baa, Baa, Black Sheep!"

Later that evening, Linda pulled out her school speller. She spread it out on the dining room table where there was lots of space, away from the family room where Grampy and Ian were watching TV. She wanted to watch TV, too, but she would never have a chance on the big spelling test next Wednesday if she didn't start on the words now.

"Big test tomorrow?" Grams asked, noticing

Linda writing each word five times on some scratch paper.

"Next week. Wednesday," Linda answered.

"Good for you for starting early. The early bird always gets the worm."

"I don't want a worm," Linda explained. "I want to get all the words right on the spelling test. After Wednesday, our class speller is going to get picked to be in the school spelling bee."

"My, wouldn't that be wonderful if you were the one picked?" Grams flitted around the room, dusting the plant stand near the window and the big hutch that contained all of her good dishes. "You a champion speller — that would give your grandfather something to think about. Something besides basketball."

Linda fidgeted in her seat. Grams just didn't understand that it wasn't as easy as all that. How could Linda ever know all the words? There were a hundred and eighty words to study!

"You were good at spelling, weren't you, Grams?"

Grams stopped dusting. "I was good at spelling." She took out paper and pencil from the hutch drawer and sat down in the chair opposite Linda to make some of her famous lists.

Grams was especially good at making lists. She wrote down lists of things to do around the house. She wrote lists of things to get Grampy to do around the house. But this list, Linda could see by sneaking a peek, was a grocery list.

Grams wrote down turkey and sweet potatoes and white potatoes and cranberries and pumpkin and oysters. Oysters? When Grams was through with her list, she marked a little check mark beside each item.

"Is that a Thanksgiving dinner list?" Linda asked.

"That's right."

"But Thanksgiving is weeks away."

"I like to do things early."

"So *you* can get a worm, too?"

Grams laughed. "So I can cook everything ahead of time and freeze it. Then your grandfather can't get into it before it's time for Thanksgiving. And when the day comes, all I have to do is thaw everything out and its ready!"

"I wish I could do that with my spelling words," Linda said thoughtfully. "I wish I could freeze them in my brain and then during the test, thaw out the ones I need."

Grams paused to consider the wish. "Is Mrs. Crandall going to give you all of the words?"

Linda shook her head. "There are too many of them. We would have to spend the whole day on spelling for her to do that."

"Then why don't you go through and study just the hard words? Make up a list of the ones you don't know very well."

It was a good idea. But Linda had an even better idea. At the back of the speller was a list of all the words from the nine weeks. If Linda could go through the big list and check off the twenty that would be on the test, then she'd have to study only those words.

How would she know which twenty Mrs. Crandall would ask for the test? She didn't. But she knew that Mrs. Crandall was a lot like Grams — she liked to check things off. And Mrs. Crandall wasn't always in the classroom when Linda arrived in the mornings. She was talking to other teachers or in the supply room down the hall. But Mrs. Crandall's spelling book would be there. And Linda guessed that Mrs. Crandall would already have the words that would be on the test checked in her book. All Linda would have to do would be to check her own list from Mrs. Crandall's. Then she would know the exact words to study.

"Linda? Didn't you hear me ask whether you want me to put marshmallows on the sweet potato casserole? If I do, I'll have to hide them from your grandfather. He'll find them and eat them up before it's time for Thanksgiving."

"Yes. Marshmallows." It was one of Linda's spelling words. She spelled it out on her paper. M-A-R-S-H-M-E-L-L-O-W-S. But it didn't look right. And she didn't feel quite right about her plan to cheat and get the word list from Mrs. Crandall's book.

She felt like a T-U-R-K-E-Y.

7

"Why walk to school when you can take the bus?" Ian asked Linda the next morning.

They had just left the house for the bus stop, only Linda had no intention of spending ten precious minutes waiting for the bus. She could walk to the school in ten minutes. And she needed those extra few minutes before the buses arrived at school to carry out her plan.

"I have something I have to do," Linda said vaguely, and she trudged off in the direction of the school. Ian shrugged his shoulders, bouncing his basketball on the ground as he shuffled in the opposite direction towards the bus stop.

Linda walked fast for the first two blocks while still in sight of Ian. After that she ran, hoping to gain even more time.

When the Riverview Elementary came into sight, Linda spotted Mrs. Crandall's blue sedan, parked in a row with the other teachers' cars. Good, she was here. But from now on, Linda would have to be very careful.

Mr. Quigley, the janitor, was just inside the door of the school. He was sweeping the front hall with a wide broom. It seemed to Linda that Mr. Quigley suddenly looked like a suspicious kind of person. Did she imagine that he had stopped sweeping to watch her after she had passed by him?

Mrs. Crandall was in her room. Linda passed right by the room and turned into the girls' bathroom. She would use the partition entry as a vantage point to keep an eye on her fourth grade classroom. That way she would know when Mrs. Crandall left the room.

Several times, Linda heard footsteps in the hall. When that happened, she dashed into the bathroom and scampered into one of the stalls to hide. Then when the footsteps went away, she paused a bit and sneaked out to the entry again, waiting for the right moment.

Finally, she caught a glimpse of Mrs. Crandall leaving the classroom. She was headed in the direction of the teachers' lounge. Now was the time. But Linda was so scared!

She heaved a deep breath and skipped out from

her hiding place and across the hall to the classroom. Urgently, she scanned Mrs. Crandall's desk for the teacher's spelling book. It was there! It was the top book in a big pile of books, as if it were waiting for her!

Linda was just about to turn the book's pages to the midterm review list when she heard footsteps in the hall.

Quick! She had to hide. She couldn't let Mrs. Crandall catch her like this!

There was no place to go, no place to hide. Linda thought about crawling under Mrs. Crandall's desk, but it would take her too long. The only alternative was to hide in the small supply closet at the side of the room.

Linda dashed to the closet, flung open the door and squeezed herself inside of it, leaving the door cracked a tiny hair, just enough to see out.

The footsteps echoed louder. Linda's heart thundered like Ian's basketball thumping against the ground. She was sure whoever was out there would hear it. If Mrs. Crandall caught her in the closet, what explanation could she give to her teacher?

"Oh, hi, Mrs. Crandall, I was practicing my disappearing act."

Or, how about the truth: "I was going to cheat by looking at your spelling book, only I didn't get a chance, so I really didn't cheat, did I?"

After a few moments which seemed like hours, Linda pressed her eye to the crack in the door and tried to peer out. There was someone in the room, all right, but she didn't think it was Mrs. Crandall.

She gently edged the door open a tiny space more, and she was right. It wasn't Mrs. Crandall in the room. It was Jill Kramer! But what was Jill doing?

Soon that became very obvious. Jill had her spelling book with her at Mrs. Crandall's desk, and she had opened Mrs. Crandall's speller, just as Linda had intended to do.

Every few seconds, Jill glanced up to look at the classroom door. Then her eyes would drop to the books and she would quickly scratch something in her book with her pencil. The stricken look on Jill's face frightened Linda as much as if *she* were the one frantically trying to check off the words at Mrs. Crandall's desk.

A breathless voice cried inside Linda, "Quit, quit, it isn't worth it! Get out of here before you get caught!"

Finally, Jill was done. She straightened Mrs.

Crandall's book back to the way it was and flopped her own speller shut. She dashed out from behind the big desk to her own desk and quickly stashed her book inside it.

That's when Linda slowly opened the closet door, stepped out and softly shut it behind her. When Jill glanced up at Linda, her face drained of all color.

The buses had arrived. Libby swung into the room, followed by Tammy and then more of the class. But Jill just kept staring at Linda.

"What's the matter with you?" Libby asked Jill.

"Oh, nothing. I think I ate my breakfast too fast."

"Why didn't you ride the bus?"

"Oh, my mother dropped me off this morning."

"You don't look too good at all, Jill. You look like a ghost."

"Maybe I had better go get a drink of water." Jill shuffled out of the room, followed by Libby and Tammy.

Linda didn't know what to do. Should she say something or just keep quiet? If she said something, whom should she say it to? Jill? Mrs. Crandall?

All day Linda wondered about the answers to

those questions, and Jill kept looking away from her. At the end of the day, after the last bell rang, Linda could stand it no longer. She had to find out what she was going to do! She ran all the way to Parmalee's.

8

The car parked squarely in front of Parmalee's ·
Diner looked like Grampy's white sedan!

Linda sneaked around the side of the car so
she wouldn't be seen, examining its hood. Sure
enough. The hood was dappled with a cat's dusty
paw prints. Those paw prints belonged to Mississippi, and the car was Grampy's!

But what was he doing at Parmalee's Diner?
Linda intended to find out.

Finally, she spotted them. Grampy and Parmalee. Sitting in one of the booths.

They were talking. Grampy had his back to
Linda, so she had no way of knowing if he was
happy or sad. Linda wondered. What could they
possibly have to talk about?

A bolt of panic shot down Linda's spine. What
if Parmalee was telling Grampy about Linda being a cheat? Grampy was nodding his head!

"No, Grampy!" Linda wanted to shout. "Don't you believe it! I'm not a cheat anymore! I only cheated that once. And, well, I was thinking about cheating again today. But I didn't! And I won't ever cheat again. Promise."

Linda studied Parmalee's face. She couldn't do it very well because she was too far away, and she only sneaked a peek when Parmalee wasn't looking out the big window that spanned the length of the diner. Parmalee was drinking a cup of coffee. In between sips of coffee, she was nodding and saying something to Grampy, looking very serious.

Linda staggered away from the car and off down the street, heading for home. How would she ever face Grampy again? How would she ever face Grampy if he knew she had cheated?

Linda kicked rocks off the sidewalk all the way up Magnolia Street. There wasn't a rock left on the sidewalk where she had been. She was going to keep kicking, but then she noticed Jill walking where the Magnolia sidewalk intersected Stucky. She was alone, and she had been crying.

"Hey, Jill!" Linda called. "What's the matter?"

Jill stopped. She glowered at Linda. "You know what's the matter," she snapped at Linda.

Linda knew that Jill had looked in Mrs. Crandall's spelling book that morning. And Jill knew she knew. Was that what she meant?

"Why are you crying?"

"It's all your fault," Jill muttered, swaying away from Linda as they met at the intersecting walk. Since they were headed in the same direction, they walked together, a big gap between them. "If you weren't so good at magic, I wouldn't have done what I did this morning."

"I'm not so good at magic," Linda admitted.

"Then you must be a fortuneteller like Parmalee. How else would you know how to spell those words on the last test? And how else would you know that if you hid in Mrs. Crandall's closet, you'd catch me copying the words?"

Jill suddenly stopped walking. Her blotchy red face was still, and then it lit up, as if a bulb in her brain had flicked on. "You cheated on that first test. And you were going to get the words from Mrs. Crandall's speller yourself!"

Linda didn't say anything. It wasn't a good feeling to be found out as a cheat. But oddly enough, she felt a sense of relief, especially since she knew Jill couldn't call her names and act high and mighty — not when Jill had done the same thing.

"This changes everything," Jill suddenly said, wiping at her eyes with renewed hope.

"What does it change?" Linda wanted to know.

"It means you probably won't be the best speller. Will you?" Then a cloud of doubt darkened Jill's face. "Oh, I get it. You got the list from Mrs. Crandall's book before I did. You only hid in the closet when you heard me coming."

"Wrong," Linda said dismally. "I was going to get the list, but you came into the room before I could copy it."

"You didn't get it?"

Linda shook her head.

"Well, that makes two of us."

"You didn't get it, either?" Linda asked, wide-eyed.

Jill shook her head.

"What did you get then?"

Jill heaved a deep breath. "I got the wrong words. Ones marked for the semester review."

"You did?"

Jill nodded and looked squarely at Linda. Linda blinked back. Then they both burst into stomach-holding laughter. Neither of them had actually cheated!

When they were finally back to normal, Jill

asked, "But what are you going to do about the test on Wednesday?"

Linda shrugged. "I've already studied most of the hard words. I guess I'll have to go back and study all the easy ones."

"You aren't going to try to get the list again?"

"No way! I was a nervous wreck just watching you trying to get the list." She studied Jill's thoughtful face. *"You* aren't going to try again to get the list, are you?"

Jill shrugged. "I'm supposed to. But I think I'll die before I try doing something like that again. I thought I was going to throw up afterward."

Linda knew just how Jill felt. But she was confused. "Why are you supposed to try?" Linda asked.

"It's what I have to do ... to join Tammy's club."

Linda was sure that Tammy was never going to ask her to join her club, but she gave her opinion anyway. "I wouldn't want to join a club that makes you do things like that."

"Oh, we aren't going to do things like this all the time. Once we are joined, we're going to do fun things. Like have sleep-overs and parties and go roller-skating."

Linda wished she could do some of those things with Jill. She wouldn't mind doing them with Libby, either. But Tammy made her nervous.

"What does Tammy have to do to join?" Linda asked, wondering.

"She doesn't have to do anything. She's the president."

"Just as I thought," Linda mumbled skeptically. "But what about Libby? Does she have to do something?"

"She said she wasn't going to do anything. She didn't even come to our meeting today."

Linda walked in silence, even though she was thinking it was pretty smart of Libby not to go to the meeting that day. And because she thought it wouldn't do her any good to study the spelling words if somebody was going to cheat on the test, she asked, "Is Tammy really going to try to find out the words Mrs. Crandall will ask on the test?"

"I don't know," Jill said. "But if Tammy wants to cheat, she'll have to do it on her own."

Linda smiled at Jill. "Good. Because I was going to ask you over to my house to study spelling tonight."

Jill's face lit up. But then she saw Tammy riding toward them on her bike. "I can't," she said.

"There you are," Tammy said, riding up to Jill. "You didn't have to run out like that."

"You didn't have to call me names."

Tammy glanced at Linda. She said, "Jill and I want to talk alone."

"No, we don't," Jill said. "Linda knows everything anyway. I told her the whole thing."

An angry look clouded Tammy's face. "Sometimes, Jill, you act like such a goose. You were the one that wanted the secret club," she complained, "and what do you do? You go tell somebody who isn't even in our club all about it."

"Nobody wants to be in your club," Linda said, gripping her school books to give her courage. "Not even Jill."

"Fine, then, I'll just worry about our girls' team winning the spelling test contest myself. Or maybe I won't worry about it at all. Maybe I'll just get a zero on my paper on Wednesday and let the boys win." Tammy planted her hands at her hips and rolled her eyes. "If *they* win the spelling bee, our class will get to do something disgusting like cut up frogs and look at their insides. I'm sure you two would just love that."

Jill looked at Linda. Linda looked at Jill. Tammy pumped angrily away on her bike.

9

Mississippi wasn't in the garage when Linda looked for him. He wasn't prowling around the yard, his whole body frozen except for the rattle-snake twitch at the end of his tail, hunting birds. Linda walked over to Bernadette's, hoping to spot the cat.

An old butter tub was turned on its side next to the bottom step of Bernadette's porch. It had been licked clean. But there was no sign of Mississippi.

Then Linda spotted something. It was a trail of blood that ended in a dark pool on the porch next to Bernadette's door.

A terrible thought poked at Linda: Bernadette couldn't be so hungry that she would eat Mississippi, would she?

She knocked at the door. "Have you seen Mississippi?" Linda skeptically eyed Bernadette through the rickety screen door. "Mississippi. The wild gray cat that lives around here?" Linda said.

Bernadette appeared to have more color in her cheeks than the day before. "Come on in." She held the door wide open for Linda to enter.

Linda smelled something different in Bernadette's house — it was something cooking. It smelled like when Grams cooked a roast. Ordinarily, she liked the smell of a roast cooking, but this time she cringed as she followed Bernadette to her kitchen.

"What's that I smell?"

"Meat."

"What kind of meat?"

"Beggars can't be choosers."

Linda stared wide-eyed at Bernadette. "You wouldn't eat just anything, would you?"

Bernadette lifted the lid of the roasting pan on the stove. "Ahh. I don't know when I've last had meat. It's been a good month or two, I know that. This is plump and juicy and freshly butchered."

Linda jumped when Bernadette clanked the lid back down on the big pot.

"I'm so hungry for a good piece of meat, I could eat a horse."

Linda stared at Bernadette in horror. If Bernadette could eat a horse, it ought to be no trouble at all for her to eat a cat.

"I have to go." Linda rushed out of the kitchen.

"Hold on a minute — I didn't have a chance to thank you."

"Thank me for what?" Linda asked.

"For the cookies and all. Can you stay to supper?" Then Bernadette's face wrinkled up. "Let's see now. There was something you asked me that I didn't answer."

"Mississippi," Linda whimpered. A shiver wriggled down her spine. Suddenly, Bernadette looked more and more like a witch. In particular, the witch in "Hansel and Gretel" that fattened poor Hansel with designs on eating him!

Linda ran out of Bernadette's house without saying another word. No wonder Parmalee hated her sister. Bernadette was a cat-eater!

Mississippi! Didn't Bernadette realize how special he was? Hadn't she ever heard him spell his name? Didn't she know he was no ordinary cat? Poor Mississippi. He never hurt anyone. He was wild and scavenged food from whoever would feed him, but he didn't deserve for Bernadette to butcher him!

Linda sped out of Bernadette's yard as fast as her legs could carry her. She dashed across the alley, zipping by the area behind the garage where Ian was dribbling his basketball. In fact, she was so scared and upset and hateful of Bernadette that she ran smack dab into Ian. He fell to the cement on his bad wrist.

Linda clapped a hand to her mouth. Oh, no! What had she done to Ian?

She stood helplessly over him as he groaned and rolled over and looked up at her with astonishment. Then his face erupted into a scowl. "Why don't you watch where you're going! Now look what you've gone and done." He held his sore wrist with his hand. "Aren't you good for anything?"

Linda mumbled that she was sorry, but Ian's malicious question choked her. She ran to the house with tears streaming down her face.

No, she wasn't good for anything. She wasn't good for saving Mississippi from a cat-eater, and she wasn't good for winning her class a party, and she wasn't good for finding out what was special about herself.

In her room, Linda cried about all of those things, her face buried in her pillow. A short while later, she felt a big hand on her shoulder.

"Hey, Lin, Lin. It's okay. Ian's going to be all right."

She wanted to say that *she* was not going to be

all right. In fact, she was going to be quite miserable for a long, long time.

"Come on, now. Grams has got supper ready on the table. You got to come eat or you know how she gets. Real insulted."

"But I can't eat, Grampy," she sniffed. "I just can't eat."

Grampy sat down on the bed and curled Linda into his arms. "Hey, now. Didn't I tell you Ian is going to be all right?"

"It's not Ian," she moaned. "It's Mississippi. Bernadette ate him."

Grampy released his grip on her so he could see her face. "Bernadette told you that?"

"No. But she has meat to eat for supper. And there was blood on her porch. And Mississippi is missing." Linda collapsed again on the bed. "She ate him!"

Grampy sat silent for a minute.

"It wasn't fair of her to do that," Linda whimpered. "Mississippi was special. He could spell his own name. He was a magical cat. I loved him. He was trying to help me find out what is special about me. And now he's gone!"

Grampy snorted. "Bernadette didn't eat that cat. That blood you saw on Bernadette's porch was blood that leaked out of a package of meat I put there."

Linda sat up, her face brightening. "But I thought you didn't like Bernadette."

"I don't like to see *anybody* go hungry."

"You were sore at me for giving her cookies."

Grampy squirmed. "I didn't give her the meat. I was just the one who delivered it."

"Then Mississippi isn't dead?"

Grampy shook his head.

Linda wiped at her eyes. "But where is he?"

Grampy sat silent a moment. "Maybe you'd better let *me* figure that out."

"On account of I'm not such a good detective?" Linda asked.

"That and a few other things," Grampy said vaguely.

Linda felt better. If Grampy would agree to find Mississippi for her, maybe he didn't hate the cat so much after all. And he had gotten her to thinking ... Why hadn't she thought of it before? She needed a detective to find out what was special about her! She didn't know any detectives, but she *did* know Libby Grimes, and Libby Grimes was pretty good at figuring things out. Linda would ask Libby what was special about her.

"Come on now. Grams has got supper ready. Come on and wash up before you and me get in trouble with the boss for being late."

Linda followed Grampy to the bathroom where they shared the lavatory, washing their hands.

"Grampy," Linda began. "Has anybody been telling you things about me?" she asked, wanting to know if Parmalee had snitched on her.

"Well, now, come to think of it, Grams has got it in her head you might be some kind of champion speller."

Linda turned away to dry her hands on a towel. And also to avoid seeing whether Grampy expected her to be a champion speller, too.

"I'm not, you know," she mumbled. "Just like Ian's not a good basketball player. *I* can shoot baskets better than him."

Grampy didn't say anything. But Linda could tell by the way he dried his big hands so slowly that he was thinking about what she said.

Linda smiled. Maybe she wouldn't be needing Libby Grimes, after all. Maybe she had made a big discovery on her own!

10

The next day at school, while they were standing in line at the water fountain, Jill whispered to Linda, "She did it!"

"Did what?"

"Copied the spelling words out of Mrs. Crandall's book."

Linda knew that Jill meant Tammy.

"Did she give them to *you?*"

Jill shook her head. "She's mad at me. But don't you see? Now, *she's* going to be the best speller because she cheated."

"Can you come to my house after school so we can decide what to do?" Linda whispered, glancing at Mrs. Crandall, who was frowning because the two girls entered the room whispering to each other.

Mrs. Crandall wasn't the only one who was upset about Jill and Linda talking together — Tammy eyed them suspiciously.

Then some really strange things happened: Jill couldn't find her pencil, or her pencil box, or the pink rabbit's foot that she kept in her desk for good luck. When Linda opened her desk lid, there they were!

Linda didn't know what to do; she hadn't been friends with Jill long enough to know whether Jill would understand that it hadn't been Linda who had put Jill's things in her own desk.

Linda didn't do anything for a while, and then she decided she'd put Jill's things back into Jill's desk when no one was looking. The only trouble was that Tammy was watching every move she made.

When Jill complained to Mrs. Crandall about her missing things, Mrs. Crandall asked the class, "Has anyone seen Jill's things?" Everyone looked blank. No one said anything. Linda knew that she should say something because she *had* seen Jill's things, but she was afraid that it would look like she had stolen them.

"Everyone look in your desks," Mrs. Crandall instructed.

The whole class looked in their desks. Then Tammy stood up, pointing at Linda's desk. "There they are, Mrs. Crandall. I see them in Linda's desk."

All eyes in the room stared at Linda. She froze. She didn't know what to do or say.

"Linda. Are Jill's things in your desk?"

Linda slowly nodded. She explained in a barely audible voice, "They weren't there when we went out to recess."

"Give them back to Jill, please." Mrs. Crandall's face sank with disappointment. Then she proceeded to lecture the class about respecting other people's property.

When Linda handed the items to Jill, Jill wouldn't look at her, even after Linda whispered, "I didn't do it!" Linda didn't ask Jill whether their plans to study spelling together after school were still on — she knew by the way Jill was acting that they were off, off, off!

After school, Linda found herself poking along the sidewalk that led to Parmalee's. She wanted to know what Parmalee would say about Tammy pulling such a dirty trick. She was sure the waitress might have some soothing words.

Grampy's car wasn't parked in front of the diner. In fact, no cars were parked there. Linda was glad; she wanted Parmalee all to herself.

When she walked in, she didn't even see Parmalee. But then she caught a glimpse of her, through the side window, waddling to the back of the diner with a bag of trash. At that moment a muffled cry seeped into the room. It sounded sort of like a baby crying from a long distance away.

Linda knew she shouldn't snoop, but the cry sounded so urgent that she walked behind the counter and down the hall that led to the back of the diner. When she pushed open the swing door at the back, she was surprised to find that Parmalee lived in three little rooms that were tacked on. There was a little living room, a bedroom, and a bathroom. In one corner of the living room was a crude wooden crate where the baby cry was coming from.

"I'm here, Linda," a voice said behind her.

Linda jumped. She could feel the blood drain from her face. "I was just . . . I was just looking . . . for you."

Parmalee nodded, satisfied with the story. But Linda knew it had looked like she was sneaking around where customers weren't supposed to go.

"I baked cinnamon rolls this morning," Parmalee said, guiding Linda back to the diner itself. "Should have saved my back. Haven't been a handful of people in today. Haven't seen you around in a while, either."

"That's because I've been having troubles of my own," Linda explained.

"Ah, yes. Somebody's been cheating again."

"You know about Tammy Collins?" Linda eyed Parmalee with greater respect. Maybe Parmalee *was* a real fortuneteller after all. Maybe that day she saw Grampy talking with Parmalee he was getting his fortune told.

"That girl needs help."

"Help! Why does Tammy Collins need help? She's got the spelling words from Mrs. Crandall's book. She's going to get a perfect spelling paper on Wednesday and then everyone will pick her to be our class speller and then she's going to choose whatever she wants for our class party!"

"Sounds like heaven, don't it, honey?" Parmalee placed a plate with a big fat cinnamon roll on it in front of Linda. Then she poured herself a cup of coffee. "Fact is, if Tammy wins at spelling, it's going to hurt her more than help her. She's going to get the notion that she can do more cheating. All she'll wind up doing is cheating herself. Cheaters don't take the time to learn anything. And then, too, someday she'll cheat when somebody won't be so kind about it as you or Mrs. Crandall. Then *wham!*"

Linda jumped. She was sure by "wham!" Parmalee meant jail, or prison, or something worse she hadn't even imagined yet. It was amazing how Parmalee could see into the future like that.

"Is there any way to stop her, to keep her from hurting herself?"

"Well, there's the hard way and the harder way." Parmalee eyed the untouched cinnamon roll on Linda's plate. Linda quickly took a bite. It tasted like scrambled eggs with spices. Linda was not fond of scrambled eggs, but she didn't say anything.

"You could study hard and do just as well on the test without cheating."

"But even if I do just as well, I haven't been here very long. The girls in my class won't pick me. They'll pick Tammy."

"What about one of the other girls? Could you help one of them win? Somebody that everyone would want to choose?"

"Jill. I could help Jill. But she's mad at me. How do you help somebody who's mad at you?"

Parmalee got this far off look on her face. "You get somebody else to be your go-between."

A sudden thought prompted Linda to ask, "Is that what you did with Bernadette? Did you get somebody to be your go-between?"

A surprised look surfaced on Parmalee's face. "I'd swear you're clairvoyant, child!"

"What's clairvoyant?"

"Able to see things others can't see. You know, like me."

"Then you *are* a fortuneteller, Parmalee. Is Bernadette clair ... clairvoyant?"

"Hummph. She tries to be. But she doesn't have the gift. She's starving herself to be what she's not cut out to be."

"And you sent her the meat," Linda said.

Again, Parmalee glanced at Linda with surprise, as if she couldn't believe Linda had figured that out on her own.

"What's the harder way of helping Tammy, Parmalee? You said there was a hard way and a harder way?"

Parmalee sipped on her coffee, studying the question. "The harder way would be for you to make things even again. Tell Mrs. Crandall that she would be wise to change her list and make sure that Tammy knows that, too."

"But I'd get called a tattletale!"

"Sometimes helping other people has risks."

The muffled baby's cry interrupted Linda's thoughts. "What's that sound, Parmalee? Did somebody leave a baby on your doorstep?"

Parmalee shook her head, eyeing Linda's cinnamon roll. "No. But I sure been left with a lot to think about." She cleared her throat and swallowed thickly. "Bernadette's not the only one doing something she's not cut out to do." She glanced away. "You best be getting along so's to get to working hard or harder on your problem. I got something of my own needs thinking on."

Taking the hint, Linda rose to leave. She didn't have to be clairvoyant to know that Parmalee needed some time alone to get used to the idea that she was not a cook but a fortuneteller.

"Look, Parmalee, magic," Linda said, making her cinnamon roll disappear from beneath a napkin she had draped over it. It was a simple trick her father had taught her. But it never failed to make an audience smile.

Parmalee pulled the cinnamon roll out of Linda's book bag, where Linda had hidden it. "What'd I tell you before about friends being friends? We don't need no tricks between us."

Linda took the cinnamon roll back from Parmalee. Then she cupped it in her hands and furled it with a perfect hook shot at the trash can near the door. It went in!

"Basket!" Parmalee said, a twinkle glinting from her eyes. "Now that's more like it!"

11

When Linda got home, Grams already had soup and sandwiches waiting. She was sniffing the air like she did when there was something she had to do but didn't really want to do it. Somehow, Grampy had convinced Grams that she should attend Ian's first basketball game.

"Basketball, smasketball." Grams swooped around the table serving supper. "How was I supposed to put a decent meal in Ian when he had to go off early like that? And who's idea was it to hold a basketball game during the dinner hour!"

Grampy looked across the table at Linda and winked. "We speak to the coaches tonight, maybe they'll change the next game just for us," he told Grams.

Linda stiffened. Already she wondered how it was that Ian was going to get to play in the game that night. She knew for a fact that he hadn't patched up his differences with Cory Richards like the coach had said. Had Grampy cheated? Had he asked the coach to let Ian play anyway?

Grams snorted. "Hush, old man, and eat your soup."

Linda ate quickly so there would be time to rush out to the garage to look for Mississippi. When she did, he wasn't there; it had been two days in a row now since she had seen any sign of him.

While she and Grampy were waiting in the car for Grams, Linda probed, "Grampy, you said you would look for Mississippi. Haven't you done anything to find him?"

"I'm working on it, Lin Lin." But he said it like he wasn't working too hard.

"I can't understand why he's not around," Linda confided. "Bernadette feeds him and ... well ... sometimes I give him a piece of cookie."

"Neither one of you should be feeding him. Bernadette 'cause she doesn't have any food to spare. And *you* 'cause those are *my* cookies."

"You don't mind sparing one cookie for a hungry cat, do you, Grampy?"

"Cookies are no food for a cat."

"Then we could start buying him cat food?"

"I didn't say that."

"But if you find him, can we buy him some food so he doesn't take all of Bernadette's?" Linda asked. Then, to point out that Grampy had probably missed out on the cat's special abilities, she said, "I bet you've never heard him spell his name, Grampy."

"I've heard him all right."

"You have? It does sound like he's spelling Mississippi, doesn't it, Grampy?"

Grampy nodded his head and smiled. "We must have the same ears, Lin Lin."

Linda looked at Grampy's ears. His were big and stuck out a bit from his head. Hers weren't that way at all. He must have meant that they heard the same. Linda wasn't sure that was true; when she brought up the subject of Mississippi, Grampy didn't seem to hear her at all.

The Riverview gymnasium was packed with people. Grampy said he'd never seen such a crowd for a sixth grade basketball game. Linda spotted Jill sitting not far from her, but Jill glanced away when Linda's eyes met hers.

Linda loped down the bleachers from where she sat with Grams and Grampy and plopped down next to Jill. "Have you decided what to do about Tammy?" she asked.

Jill shrugged. She scooted away from Linda. When Linda scooted closer to Jill, Jill turned to Linda and blurted out, "Why did you take my things?"

"I didn't."

"But they were in your desk."

"Only because Tammy put them there."

Jill looked straight ahead. Both of them watched as the Riverview team, wearing gold and blue uniforms, bounded down the court to the Riverview basket. Linda still couldn't believe it. Ian was playing!

Instead of passing the ball to others on the team, Ian kept it to himself. When he tried shooting it, he was too far away from the goal. The ball bounced off the rim of the basket and the other team grabbed it and raced back to the other end.

"Who is that boy? The one that won't pass the ball to anyone else?" Jill thought out loud.

"He's my brother," Linda admitted quietly.

Jill glanced sideways at Linda. "What's wrong with him?"

Linda shrugged, a little embarrassed. "He hurt his wrist," she tried to explain. But it didn't really explain how Ian was acting.

Jill gasped as they witnessed another attempt by Ian to hog the ball. Rushing another shot, Ian's toss fell short of the basket again.

"He must be nervous," Linda continued to explain. "First game and all."

"Look," Jill pointed out, "the coach is taking him out."

It was true. A buzzer sounded, and the Riverview coach motioned to Ian to sit on the bench. Another player took Ian's place. Ian stomped off the gym floor and kicked at a towel lying in front of the bench. He kicked and kicked at it. Linda had never seen Ian behave like such a raging bull. She was glad when the game resumed and everyone seemed to forget about Ian.

"We can't let Tammy cheat on the test on Wednesday," Jill said. "If she gets a perfect paper, she'll get picked as our girl speller. And if that happens, she won't be the best person to be our speller in the bee."

"But what can we do?" Linda wanted to know.

Jill shrugged. She knew the problem, but she didn't have any solutions.

They sat silently watching as the Riverview team worked the ball down the floor to their goal, passing it from player to player, edging it closer to the basket.

"We've all got to study for that test," Linda blurted out to Jill. "And the best speller should be the one to be in the bee."

Jill nodded. "But that might not stop Tammy."

Linda knew what had to be done to stop Tammy from cheating. Mrs. Crandall would have to be told that her list of words was no good anymore — then she could change her list, and everybody would be even again.

"Somebody'll have to tell Mrs. Crandall," Linda said.

"Somebody could leave a note on her desk," Jill suggested.

"But then Tammy wouldn't know that Mrs. Crandall had been told. She'd study only the words from the list."

Linda thought hard again. "I know. Somebody could go in early tomorrow and write the message to Mrs. Crandall on the front blackboard. That way Mrs. Crandall and the whole class would know. Including Tammy," Linda said.

"Good. It's a good idea." But Jill frowned. "Who's going to do it?"

Linda shrank down on the bleacher. "Not me. If Tammy ever found out I did it, she'd put something worse than your things in my desk."

Jill laughed. Linda was relieved that Jill understood it was Tammy who had taken her things. She was uncomfortable, though, thinking about what Tammy might do to the person who wrote the message on the blackboard.

"I can't write the message," Jill explained. "I have a dentist appointment first thing in the morning. I'll be late getting to school."

Linda knew that meant that *she* would have to write the message on the blackboard. And with Jill gone, Tammy would know for sure it was her! "But *I* can't do it. What if I get caught? What if Mrs. Crandall catches me and questions me? I can't lie!"

"It won't take you long to write a few words on the blackboard," Jill argued.

"But what if Tammy guesses? She's going to think either you or I did it. And if you come to school an hour later, she'll know for sure it was me. We're the only ones that know about her cheating to get the list."

Jill seemed to understand perfectly that what Linda needed was some sign that they were going to stick together. "Want to form a special club for members that want to do fun things together?"

Linda smiled and nodded. Those words were magic to her ears.

12

No one said anything all the way home from the basketball game — even Grams was silent. But after Grampy eased the car into the garage, Ian was the first to hop out. In passing, he kicked the front car tire. He kicked Grampy's saw table. He kicked the garage door!

Linda was glad that Mississippi was not in the garage. Ian might have tried to kick *him*. And that's when a light bulb clicked on in her brain. Ian *had* kicked Mississippi before! She knew it! She knew it! That was why Mississippi was so afraid of people!

She hated Ian for kicking Mississippi. She hated him for acting the way he was acting. So it wasn't easy living in a new place away from their parents, but it was what Ian had wanted!

Ian was having a bad time fitting in and troubles playing basketball — did he have to take it out on Mississippi? No, he did not! And she was going to make sure that he never kicked Mississippi again. If and when she could ever find the cat . . .

Without even asking permission, Linda ran out the garage door, across the alley, and over to Bernadette's house. It was dark in the yard, and no lights were on inside the big house. Had Bernadette gone to bed so early? It was barely nine o'clock.

Peeking in the big double windows at one side of the house, Linda spotted Bernadette sitting at the dining room table. She was trying to read a book by the light of a candle. Linda knocked on the door.

"Have you seen Mississippi today?"

Bernadette peered out at Linda with a dejected look. "Mississippi? Oh, the cat. I can't feed him anymore."

"I know, Bernadette, but did he come around today? Did he come begging for food?"

"Only the electricity man came today. He shut off my power."

"Why did he do that?"

"I couldn't pay my bill."

Linda felt embarrassed for Bernadette. "Is he going to come turn it back on again?"

"Not without money."

"Can't you get a job? You could get a job cooking, Bernadette. You're a wonderful cook."

"Oh, no. I can't do that. I can't get a job cooking."

"Why not?"

"Because of a pledge Parmalee and I made."

"What kind of pledge?"

"She doesn't tell fortunes and I don't cook. That way we don't get in each other's way."

Linda thought about the pledge for a moment. It was all mixed up. Parmalee should be the one telling fortunes, and Bernadette should be the one cooking food. How did they ever get so switched? She asked Bernadette.

"It comes from being twins," Bernadette explained. "We look alike, so people got us confused. So half the time, people were thinking Parmalee was the one cooking good food. And she started believing it. And the other half of the time, people thought I was the one who could tell fortunes. It got us so mixed up betwixt ourselves that we started fighting over which one of us people were talking about when they said good things."

"So you had a big fight?"

Bernadette nodded. "And we've never been the same since. We've never even spoken. Except to say that she's supposed to be the cook, since she has the diner, and I'm supposed to tell the fortunes, since I have this house. Only I don't think I'm going to have this house much longer."

Linda glanced down, embarrassed for Bernadette again. "Shouldn't you talk to Parmalee? Shouldn't you two trade places before both of you starve?"

Bernadette sighed. "It's not as simple as that."

Linda was beginning to believe nothing was simple — she had lost Mississippi, Ian was acting so terrible, and then there was the spelling problem at school.

"I did see something strange the other day," Bernadette offered.

"What? What did you see?"

"I saw a young boy chase the cat clear across the alley into my yard."

"That was my brother, Ian," Linda explained. "He's been mean to Mississippi all along, only I didn't know it."

"Your grandfather knew it."

"Grampy?"

Bernadette nodded.

Grampy would stop Ian's cruelty to Mississippi, wouldn't he? Linda wondered. "I've got to go," she said quickly, wheeling around on the porch and running down off of it. In the dark, she streaked across Bernadette's yard, darted across the alley, and zipped through the back yard to the house.

Ian was in his room. He had the door closed. Linda knocked.

"Go away. I don't want to talk to anybody."

"It's me, Ian."

"Go away."

Linda turned the knob. The door wasn't locked, so she gently cracked it to peer in at Ian. He was lying across his bed, a pillow flopped over his head.

"Why, Ian?" she began. "Why were you mean to Mississippi?"

Ian lifted one side of the pillow and peered out at her with a scowling look. "Mississippi who?" he growled.

"Mississippi, my cat. Why did you kick him and chase him and make him afraid of people?"

"That stupid old cat?"

"He's not stupid! He's my friend, and you treated him horribly."

"That's just a dumb old stray cat. Go away! Can't you see I have more important things to think about than some dumb old stray cat?"

Linda stayed put. "I want to know what you

did with him. He's missing. Something happened to him. I want to know right now!"

Ian shoved the pillow away from his head with disgust. "I made a fool out of myself tonight playing basketball and you're worried about that stupid cat?"

Linda scowled back at Ian. "What did you do with him?"

A devilish grin wormed its way to Ian's lips. "Maybe I hung him from a tree."

Linda gasped.

"Maybe I buried him alive."

Linda grabbed the pillow off of Ian's head and hit him with it.

"Maybe I sawed him in half with Grampy's saw."

Now Linda was pounding Ian so hard and with such vigor that she felt she couldn't stop. A large hand caught hers in midair.

"That's not going to solve anything," Grampy said. He loosened the pillow from Linda's grasp and guided her to the door.

"He's done something with Mississippi, Grampy, and he won't tell me what," Linda whimpered, tears pooling in her eyes.

Outside Ian's door, Grampy said, "He's only

telling you all those things to rile you up, Lin Lin. He's striking out at you because he's really angry about something else — playing bad basketball. He hasn't done anything to that cat."

"No, but *you* did," Ian said, accusing Grampy from his doorway.

Linda looked at Ian and then at Grampy. Grampy's face stiffened, as if Grams had caught him with his hand in the cookie jar. No, not Grampy! Grampy couldn't have done something mean and cruel to Mississippi. Otherwise, how would she ever know what to believe anymore?

One thing was for sure: neither Ian nor Grampy was going to tell her the truth. She would have to find it out on her own.

She ran to her own bed and smothered her head with pillows, just like Ian, but with one exception: before she did, she locked the door.

13

When Mrs. Crandall walked into the classroom the next morning, she paused, along with the whole class, to read the message drawn in big white letters on the green chalkboard at the front of the room:

"SOMEONE IN THIS ROOM KNOWS WHAT SPELLING WORDS MRS. CRANDALL IS GOING TO ASK."

Mrs. Crandall erased the board. Then she turned and faced her students. "Let me assure you, class, that no one knows what words I will ask on the test tomorrow. And that is because I intend to compile a whole new list of words."

No one said anything. Tammy Collins, however, raised her hand.

"Mrs. Crandall. I think I know who wrote that on the board."

Linda froze in her seat.

Mrs. Crandall slowly shook her head. "It really

doesn't matter who wrote that on the board, Tammy. Whoever wrote it believed that someone was going to cheat on the test tomorrow. And now everyone knows there is no chance of anyone doing that."

Tammy's face fell. She glared at Linda. Linda sank down in her chair, eyeing Jill's empty chair in front of her. Why did Jill have to have a dentist appointment today of all days? She had never felt so alone in all her life!

She had never felt like such a cornered animal, either. When she returned to her seat from sharpening her pencil, she found a wad of chewed gum on her chair. Libby noticed it, too, and she whisked out a tissue from her desk and wiped up the gum for Linda. Then she dropped the sticky blob on top of Tammy's desk. Right smack-dab in the middle of the math paper Tammy was working on!

Nothing else happened after that, but at morning recess, Tammy cornered Linda outside the school door. "You think you're so smart. Go ahead. Be the best speller tomorrow. But I'll make sure nobody votes for you to be in the spelling bee. Getting all the words right won't do you a bit of good."

Tammy marched off to gather her friends around her in the playground. Linda knew they were talking about her. She went back inside the school and hung around the front doors, hoping Jill would come from the dentist.

At lunch time, Jill was still not at school. Linda let other kids go ahead of her in the lunch line in hopes that Jill would come and they could eat together. A lot of good that did — Tammy nudged past where Linda was standing in line and handed her half of a banana from her tray, which had been part of her lunch. "Here, Monkeyface."

Linda stood there with the banana in her hand as Tammy and the other girls' laughter echoed in her ears. She wanted to throw that banana at Tammy, but Mrs. Crandall was watching, so she simply dropped it in the trash, her face burning with embarrassment.

After playing alone during noon recess, Linda found something on her desk when she came back into the classroom. It was a note. She knew she shouldn't read it, but she did anyway. It was the cruelest joke of the whole day.

"WHY DON'T YOU AND YOUR WHOLE FAMILY DIS-APPEAR?"

Linda fought back the tears. She wadded up the

note and shoved it into her desk. She hated Tammy Collins. She hated this school and living with Grams and Grampy and Ian for being so mean. She hated Jill for not coming today to help her. She wanted to run away!

The rest of the afternoon dragged by. Finally, the last bell rang. Linda waited till all of the others left before she ambled out the classroom door. And even that didn't do her any good, because Tammy was waiting for her again!

"You'd better not have a perfect spelling paper tomorrow if you know what's good for you."

Linda didn't know where her voice came from or what gave her the courage to say it, but she had had enough trouble with Tammy Collins. "I know what's good for me. You're the one who needs a spelling lesson. Scram. S-C-R-A-M!"

Tammy looked at her really funny, as if she'd been slapped in the face or something. Her mouth dropped open and she couldn't seem to move.

Linda loped out of the school. She felt better than she'd felt all day. She felt like she could do anything! She could run faster than anybody. She could spell better than anybody! She might even be able to eat Parmalee's food without gagging!

She dashed inside the diner. "Look at my face,"

she told Parmalee. "See anything written all over it?"

Parmalee studied Linda for a moment. "By gosh, I think I do. There's something different about you today."

"I just stood up to Tammy Collins. She bothered me all day, until finally I told her she'd better quit."

"Did she?"

"From the look on *her* face, she's going to." Then a sinking feeling began to wash over Linda. Tammy might have been stunned by Linda's talking back to her, but no, she probably wasn't going to stop bothering her altogether.

"What's the matter?" Parmalee sensed that something was suddenly wrong.

"It's not going to work." Linda sank down in one of the diner booths. "Even if I study really hard and get the best grade on the spelling test, Tammy has too many friends who won't vote for me to be in the bee."

Parmalee rubbed her face. "Well, now. Maybe that isn't what you should worry about. Maybe first you ought to worry about why you want to win that chance to be in the spelling bee in the first place."

Linda thought long and hard for a moment. Why *did* she want to be in the bee? Why does anyone want to be picked for something special? ... Because they want to be singled out. Linda wanted to be admired and looked up to, to shine like a star. She wanted to be like her parents; she wanted to show that she could also do something extraordinary, like them. She told all those things to Parmalee.

Parmalee nodded slowly in agreement. "But I think maybe you're missing the point of this spelling business. You're losing sleep about how you're going to come out looking to other people. Is this here bee going to make you feel better about yourself?"

Parmalee certainly came up with tough questions!

"It's time I showed you something." The waitress heaved herself up from the booth and motioned for Linda to follow her. They walked behind the counter and down the hall that led to Parmalee's little apartment.

Linda knew the moment she heard the cry clearly that it was Mississippi. He was here! In Parmalee's tiny living room! And he was housed in a crude wooden box that Grampy had nailed together. He meowed, and he hissed twice, but he didn't snort.

"Mississippi! What is he doing here?"

"Your grandpa brought him here."

"Why?"

"Two reasons: so Bernadette would stop sharing her food with the cat, and so your brother wouldn't have nothing to kick around when his temper got out of hand."

"But why didn't Grampy tell me?"

"Guess maybe he had the notion you wouldn't understand."

"I don't understand, Parmalee."

"You might think he was getting rid of the cat because you think he doesn't like it. He was afraid you'd confuse his reasons. But he still did it because he knew it was the best thing for the cat, even if it made him appear like a traitor to you."

"That's what I thought, all right," Linda admitted.

"Well, now you know that's not the reason." She winked. "And now your grandpa knows he's got to risk doing the right thing even if it disappoints you and Ian from time to time."

Linda nodded. "But what are *you* going to do with Mississippi, Parmalee?"

"Lordy, I don't know. I just know he can't stay in this cage all the rest of his life. You've got to come after school from now on and see if you can tame this critter. Otherwise, no telling what's going to have to happen to him."

"I'll come," Linda promised. "And if I can tame Mississippi, I'd be doing it for him instead of myself, wouldn't I, Parmalee? So he wouldn't have to stay in the crate? I'd be doing the same as Grampy?"

Parmalee nodded. "You and that grandpa of yours show a lot of resemblance to each other."

Linda smiled. It was what she'd been thinking all along. But it was good to hear Parmalee say it.

14

There was a boy on the front porch when Linda got home. He was tall and skinny with big hands that he kept dipping in and out of his jacket pockets.

"You Ian's sister?" he called to Linda when he noticed her walking up.

Linda nodded.

"How come there's nobody home?"

Linda shrugged. She was a little nervous talking to this boy. He seemed intent on doing something, but nobody being home had changed his plans, making him more antsy than before.

"Well, when will Ian be back?"

Linda shrugged again. "Why do you want him?"

"We got something to settle."

"Are you mad at him?"

"That's none of your business."

Linda's eyes widened. Whatever the boy wanted to see Ian about, it was not something friendly. "You want a cookie while you wait?" she asked, hoping to soften the boy's temper.

"I'm starved. But I wouldn't take nothing from Ian Cappanelli. Not if it was the last thing on earth!"

"Oh, the cookies don't belong to Ian," Linda explained. "They belong to Grampy. Only he isn't really supposed to eat cookies." She motioned to the boy. "Follow me."

He trailed her around to the back of the house and to the garage. He watched her, wide-eyed, as she pulled down the stepladder from where it hung on the garage wall, unfolded it, climbed three rungs, reached up, and brought down a new package of Krispy Krunches.

"You Cappanellis are strange. Most people keep cookies in a cookie jar in the house."

Linda laughed as she ripped open the new package and extended it to the boy. "What's your name?"

"Cory Richards."

"O-hh. Cory Richards."

"Something wrong with my name?"

Linda shook her head. "Nothing at all. But now

I know who you are. You're the boy that Ian got in a fight with."

"I didn't pick that fight!"

Linda handed him another cookie. "You said Ian was a cheat."

"What would *you* call it when a player gets to play just because his grandfather talks to the coach?"

"But I was at the game the other night," Linda argued. "Ian got taken out of the game."

"That was because he wouldn't let anyone else near the ball. Coach had no choice."

"I know." Linda glanced down. "Why do you suppose Ian acted that way?"

"I don't know and I don't care," Cory said. "All I know is Ian didn't tell Coach I apologized to him for fighting. But I *did* apologize. I want to play, don't I?"

Linda shrugged. "If you say so." After holding out a handful of cookies for Cory and taking a handful for herself, she replaced the cookies above the garage opener and put away the ladder. Then she took down Ian's basketball from the holder Grampy had made to keep it on. She tossed it to Cory. "You want to shoot some baskets?"

Cory nodded.

They went out to the cement behind the garage. Cory dribbled the ball and then arced it high in the air at the basket. It bounced off the rim and shot over to Linda.

Linda automatically grabbed the ball and dribbled it in front of her, although it almost hit her in the face because she wasn't used to dribbling a ball.

"Shoot!" Cory urged.

Linda shot. The ball sailed through the air and sank through the hoop.

"Where'd you learn to shoot like that?" Cory asked with surprise.

"Nowhere. Ian never lets me play with him."

"I'm not surprised," Cory said about Ian. "He's a hog. But you play like a cat. Smooth and swift," he said.

They took turns passing the ball back and forth and shooting. When Linda had made five baskets to Cory's three, Cory said, "I've never seen anybody shoot like that. You must have some kind of natural ability. You play really good for a girl."

That was a compliment, Linda wondered, wasn't it? She thought Cory meant it as a compliment, anyway.

"Are you good at spelling?" Linda asked Cory.

Cory shook his head. "I have to study really hard. Even then, I'm not much good."

"Me either," Linda admitted. "But there's this spelling test tomorrow. I have to do well on it."

Cory paused to fish out another cookie from his jacket pocket. He popped it in his mouth and started chewing. "Why don't you ask Ian to help you?"

"Ian?"

"Yeah. He's the best speller in our class. We picked him to be in the school spelling bee."

"Ian? My brother, Ian?"

Cory nodded. Then he glanced at his watch. "I got to get home." He bounced the ball to Linda. "You ought to think about trying out for a team." Then, somewhat grumpier, he said, "Tell Ian I'll talk to him at school tomorrow."

Linda nodded and watched him stride away. She shot another basket. It went in!

Soon Grampy's car pulled up in the alley and eased inside the garage. Ian was out of the car and grabbing the ball out of Linda's hand before she could finish her cookie.

"Who said you could play with my ball?"

"I didn't think you would mind. You weren't using it."

"Well, I *do* mind. Don't ever use it again!"

Linda walked off to the back yard fence and eyed Ian. Her brother was one of the best sixth-grade spellers? She still couldn't believe it.

"Ian? You think you could help me with something?"

"Why should I?"

"Because you're the best person to help me."

"With what?"

"Spelling."

"Who told you I was good at spelling?"

"You *were* chosen as one of the best sixth-grade spellers, weren't you?"

"Oh, that," Ian waved her away. "Who cares about that?"

"I do! Why didn't you tell anybody you'd been picked as one of the best sixth-grade spellers?"

"It's just something that happened. No big deal."

"No big deal?" Grampy waddled out from the garage. "You gonna deprive me and your grandmother of something to brag about?"

"It's not as good as basketball."

"And who says?"

"I don't know," Ian said, slowing his dribbling of the ball. "You've always wanted me to play basketball."

Grampy rubbed the back of his neck. "If you wanted to. But, hey, that spelling is a real honor. Your mom and dad are going to be so proud when they hear."

Ian rolled his eyes. "Just because I'm going to be in some dumb spelling bee doesn't mean anything. I haven't won anything."

"Well, we'll be rooting for you. Won't we, Linda?"

Linda stiffened. How could she root for Ian in that bee if she hoped to be in it herself? But she knew Grampy needed her to say she would root for Ian; and Ian needed her to say it worse than Grampy did. "Yeah, Grampy. We'll be rooting for Ian."

Ian grinned. "I guess I could help you out with spelling tonight," he said to Linda.

Linda watched the ball fly in a high arc toward the basket. She heard the groan that escaped Ian when the ball whacked the backboard and shot away from the basket, missing again.

15

Jill Kramer was lurking by the front door when Linda walked into school the next morning. Jill's hand covered her mouth. When Linda said hello, Jill mumbled something from beneath her hand.

"Why didn't you come yesterday?"

Jill took her hand away. She said three words that all sounded alike, talking with her lips pinched together. In response to the confused look on Linda's face, Jill grabbed Linda's hand and pulled her along the hall to the girls' bathroom. Only when Jill was sure no one else was in the bathroom did she talk normally. "I got braces!"

She made a fish face to show a row of metal kinks spanning her upper teeth.

"Wow, does it hurt?"

Jill shook her head. "Only a little."

"It took all day to get that on you?"

Jill shook her head again. Linda suspected that

Jill planned to do a lot of head shaking instead of talking. "I didn't want everybody looking at me when I came back to school. I only came today because my mom made me."

"How long do you have to wear them?"

Jill shrugged. "Probably a year."

Linda said, "You can't hide out for a year. You've got to be our class speller!"

"Why?"

"Because you're the best speller in the class."

"But I can't stand up in front of the whole school with braces on my teeth. It's going to be hard enough just wearing them in our class."

"Well, *I* can't be our class speller."

"Why not? Didn't you study?"

"I studied. But even if I get all the words right, the rest of the girls won't pick me. And even if they did, my brother is one of the sixth-grade spellers."

"He is?"

Linda nodded. "You have to be the speller. And anyway, by next Monday, when the spelling bee is held, you'll be used to your braces."

"I'll never be used to these braces," Jill moaned, making faces at herself in the bathroom mirror.

Mrs. Crandall smiled at Jill when the two of

them entered the classroom. Jill didn't smile back.

Tammy was already in her seat, but Jill didn't look at her. Linda noticed that it didn't take Tammy long to figure out there was something wrong with Jill — Tammy had a sixth sense about other people's weak spots.

"Hey, everybody, Jill has braces!"

Suddenly the whole class turned and stared at Jill. Jill shrunk down in her chair.

Linda sighed; thanks to Tammy, now she would never be able to convince Jill to be in the spelling contest.

"All right, class, let's get ready for the spelling test," Mrs. Crandall said.

Thank goodness for Mrs. Crandall.

"I'm so glad *I* don't have to wear braces," Tammy called to Libby, who was sitting in front of her. "They make Jill look like a robot."

Linda glared across the aisle at Tammy. "We're glad you don't have to wear braces, either. Your mouth is so big the dentist would have to put an oil derrick in there!"

Tammy gasped. "You'd better watch what you say, Monkeyface."

"Same to you," Linda whispered back. She meant to say more, but Mrs. Crandall's eyebrows lifted. She was ready to call out the words.

Linda took out a sheet of paper and numbered it from one to twenty. The first three words were easy, but she knew Mrs. Crandall was going to get to the tough ones pretty soon. By the eighth word, she was right. Did "community" have two m's or one? Linda realized that she wasn't the only one wondering — when she glanced sideways, she caught Tammy trying to peek at her paper.

She wondered: Is it cheating to write down the wrong answer if you know it is wrong so somebody copying off of you will get it wrong, too?

Even though Linda knew better, she put only one m in "community." She spelled "director" with an er instead of an or. She smiled at Tammy when Mrs. Crandall pronounced "beast." Linda spelled the word B-E-E-S-T. Tammy fell right into the trap. She copied the word from Linda's paper, letter by letter.

At the end of the twenty words, the girls exchanged papers with the boys and Mrs. Crandall spelled out the correct spelling of each word while the class graded the papers.

Linda watched Tammy when Mrs. Crandall spelled out the three words Linda had purposefully written wrong. Tammy's face sagged.

After tabulating the scores of the spelling papers, Mrs. Crandall called out, "This has been a very close contest. But it looks like the girls have finished ahead of the boys."

All the girls in the room cheered, and the boys groaned. Tammy waved her arm. "Mrs. Crandall, can the girls decide who to pick as our speller now?"

Mrs. Crandall smiled. "Yes, Tammy. But it might be helpful to know that Jill Kramer has the best record of all the girl spellers. Jill had a perfect paper today."

Although Linda couldn't see Jill's face, she knew she must be smiling, braces or no braces.

"But we don't *have* to pick *her,* do we?" Tammy wanted to know.

Mrs. Crandall frowned. "I would think you would want to choose your best speller, wouldn't you?"

"But how can we know who the best speller is?" Tammy continued, "if somebody cheated?"

Mrs. Crandall's face drained of color. "That's a very serious accusation, Tammy," she finally said. "I will look over all of the papers and decide on this tomorrow."

Mrs. Crandall stiffly collected the papers. Linda turned to Tammy and cast her a disgusted scowl. What did Tammy Collins mean by telling Mrs.

Crandall somebody cheated on the test? Tammy was the only one who cheated! Off of Linda!

"What happened?" Jill asked at recess. When Linda told her how she had tricked Tammy by writing some of her words wrong, Jill's mouth dropped open. She forgot all about her braces. "She's trying to get me in trouble," Jill decided. "So I won't be the girl speller."

"How's she going to do that?" Linda asked.

Jill's face sank. "She's going to tell Mrs. Crandall I copied the words from Mrs. Crandall's book."

"But you didn't! Not the right ones, anyway."

Jill shrugged. "She'll probably forget to tell *that* part of it."

"Maybe I should talk to Mrs. Crandall," Linda offered. "I'm a witness. I can tell Mrs. Crandall you copied the wrong words."

Jill shook her head slowly. "That'll only make Tammy tell on *you.*"

"You told Tammy I cheated on the first test?"

Jill glanced down at the ground, and Linda knew that Jill had told about her cheating. When Jill looked back up, Linda shrugged to let her know she was not angry. "Tammy is not going to stop stirring things up until she gets to pick the class speller. I think she wants to be the speller herself. She may even tell Mrs. Crandall that *I* copied off of her today instead of her copying off of me," Linda said, sighing. "I guess I'd better tell Mrs. Crandall about cheating on the first test before Tammy does. I wish I had never cheated on that first test."

"Me, too. And you know what? I wish you didn't cheat on this test, either."

"Cheat! I didn't cheat. Tammy was the one who cheated."

Jill shrugged. "You cheated yourself. Aren't you always going to wonder what might have happened if you spelled the words for real? You might have been chosen as the girl speller. Now there's no way for sure you'll ever know."

Linda looked away from Jill. Her friend was right.

16

All day long, Linda couldn't get the spelling test out of her mind — all day she wondered what would have happened if she had spelled those three words right.

She would have gotten a perfect paper, that was for sure, but would Tammy have gotten a perfect paper, too, when she cheated off of Linda? Then what would have happened?

"Hey, Cappanelli!" a voice called to her as she was leaving the school at the end of the day.

It was Cory Richards!

Linda waited by the door until Cory caught up with her. "What to come shoot some baskets?"

Linda's eyes widened. "Now? In the gym?" She said that because Cory was holding a basketball and his head was leaning toward the gym door. "Don't you have basketball practice?"

"Before practice. I told Coach Milgram about you. He wants to see you shoot."

Linda froze. She couldn't go shoot baskets for Coach Milgram. What if Ian saw her there?

"I can't."

Cory frowned. "But I told the coach. Nobody else will be there but us."

"But what about Ian?"

"What about him?"

"He wouldn't like it."

Cory shrugged. "Ian quit the team."

"He quit? Why?"

Cory glanced down at the ground. "Coach had a long talk with him. He told Ian that he had to think about whether basketball was something he really wanted to do. I think he quit because he figured out basketball just isn't his game."

Linda studied Cory's face. Now she could see how hard it had been for Cory to say something to the coach about her. The least Linda could do was to go talk to the coach.

"All right. But I can't stay long."

She followed him to the gym. Surprisingly, it was quiet there. All the boys were in the locker room suiting up for practice. Coach Milgram smiled at her.

"Understand you're a good basketball player, Linda."

Linda blushed. "I haven't had much practice."

Coach Milgram bounced the ball to her. "Let me see you shoot."

Linda shot the ball from the free-throw line. The ball sank into the basket. She shot from the sides and from different angles. All of her shots swished through the net.

"That's good shooting," the coach said when she was finished. "Let me see you dribble."

Linda dribbled around the court. At first, the ball kept hitting her in the face, but after a while, she could walk while dribbling the ball. It would take a lot more practice for her to run and dribble at the same time.

"Want to practice with us?" Coach Milgram asked when he had seen enough. "You need a lot more work, but you have the potential to be a good basketball player. Of course, since you're only in fourth grade, you wouldn't get to play in any of the sixth-grade games. The other teams we play might call that unfair," he joked.

Linda beamed, then hesitated. "But this is a boys' team."

"It's only a boys' team because we don't have any girls who want to play. There's no rule that says it has to have only boys."

Linda beamed again. She wanted to play more than anything, but did she dare?

"What about my brother? Ian? He's not going to like it if I practice with this team."

Coach Milgram shrugged. "That's something you'll have to settle with your brother yourself. Ian doesn't play on this team anymore. He's better suited to something that doesn't require a team effort. Some people are like that. It doesn't make them better or worse than anybody else. Just different."

"But how would you know I'm not like my brother? How would you know I'm a team player or if I'm better at doing something by myself?"

"I wouldn't," the coach said. "Guess we would have to find that out."

"I'll have to think about it," Linda said. She slowly walked toward the gym door. When she turned to look back, Cory Richards waved at her. She waved back.

"You seem different today," Parmalee said when Linda walked into the diner. "Something happen I don't know about?"

Linda laughed. Parmalee was supposed to know things before somebody told her. But Parmalee would never guess that Cory Richards had asked her to try out for basketball practice. She wished she could talk to Parmalee about it, so that maybe she could help her make up her mind about playing basketball. But she couldn't tell *anyone* about it. It was a secret she wanted to keep a while longer.

"Jill Kramer is going to get picked as our class speller," Linda announced to Parmalee. "Mrs. Crandall said Jill should be the one who is picked."

Parmalee was silent for a few minutes. Then she changed the subject. "Want to see Mississippi?"

Linda nodded. She followed Parmalee back to her tiny apartment. Mississippi wasn't in the wooden crate! He was sitting in the window, watching the bird action outside. He meowed and hissed. But he hissed only once this time.

Ordinarily, it would have made Linda happy that Mississippi was getting more relaxed around people, but she sensed that Mississippi's improvement came from Parmalee's misfortune. "You've been working with him a lot," she said.

Parmalee shrugged. "Nothing much else around here to do."

"Still no customers?"

"A few here, a few there. Mostly coffee drinkers."

"I saw a fancy car pull away out front just before I came in," Linda observed.

"That was no customer," Parmalee explained.

"That was the banker who holds the mortgage on this place. Looks like I have two weeks to turn this place around or lose it."

"Oh, Parmalee," Linda groaned. She edged closer to Mississippi and dared to stroke the fur of the cat. Mississippi didn't cry out or object to her touch! "Isn't there anything you can do?"

Parmalee slumped down in the easy chair. "You'd have thought with me being as good as I am at predicting the future, I would have seen this coming." A chuckle rumbled out of her chest. "Guess maybe I'm no good at telling my own fortune."

"I can tell it, Parmalee." Linda lifted Mississippi off the window sill and carried him to the tiny couch, where she sat down. "Your luck is going to change, Parmalee. I can feel it. Something good is going to happen."

"Well, it better happen soon. But just in case, maybe you better take that cat home with you today. I'm getting to the point where I can't even feed a cat."

Linda thought about Ian kicking Mississippi. He was bound to kick Mississippi again if he found out Linda was considering playing basketball. She couldn't bring Mississippi back home yet — not until she was able to make some decisions. She told Parmalee why she couldn't take Mississippi with her.

Parmalee looked at her with a confused expression. "My powers must be ebbing out of me the same way as I'm losing all my business."

"Why do you say that, Parmalee?"

"I keep getting these strong vibes about you. Darned if they don't keep telling me you've got something to do with that spelling bee."

Linda wished Parmalee hadn't said that. Now *she* was confused.

17

When Linda got home, she spotted Bernadette digging in her garden again, scavenging for more carrots. That could mean only one thing: Bernadette was hungry.

Linda ran to Grams's freezer. There were mountains of food in there...rolls and coffee cakes and pies and Thanksgiving dressing! Linda filled her arms with some of each. She was about to top it all off with a container of Grams's famous clam chowder when a big hand clamped her arm.

"Hold on there, Lin Lin. My cookies are one thing. You give away Thanksgiving and I'm the one who'll get scalped."

"But Grampy, it's for Bernadette. She's going hungry again."

Grampy studied Linda's face for a moment. "Cheating one person to give something to another never solves anything. A person just winds up cheating himself."

120

Linda knew Grampy was right. Hadn't she found that out when she caused Tammy to miss those spelling words? She put the food back in the freezer. Actually, she felt relieved not to have to cheat Grams out of the food she'd spent days baking. But what was Grampy going to do — ask Parmalee for more meat for Bernadette? This time, Linda knew for a fact that Parmalee didn't have any food to spare for Bernadette.

"What's going to happen to Bernadette, Grampy?"

"What's going to happen to you if you keep sneaking?"

"But I was only trying to help."

"There are ways of helping that don't have anything to do with cheating," Grampy argued.

Linda's eyes studied the floor. She supposed he was right in calling her a cheat. And maybe she was never going to be anything but a cheat for her whole life!

Tears stung her eyes. Grampy's big hand cupped her chin and lifted it up. "Something else is bothering you, Lin Lin."

Linda nodded. Through sniffles, she told Grampy about cheating on the first spelling test. She told him about cheating Tammy Collins by purposefully spelling three words wrong. She told

121

him how much she wanted to play basketball, only she couldn't, because Ian was supposed to be the basketball player in the family and she'd be cheating him if she played, wouldn't she?

Grampy lifted her up and sat her down on the chest freezer so they could talk eye to eye. "You're getting your cheating all mixed up, Lin Lin. Playing basketball wouldn't be cheating Ian. Just because he tried it out and found out it wasn't for him . . . well, that doesn't mean you shouldn't have your chance."

Linda wiped her eyes with her sleeve. "Then I should play?"

"Depends on what you want to do. But if you do play, you have to give it all you got. And you can't let anybody else on that team influence the way you play. It has to be your best or nothing. There'd be a whole team counting on you, even if it's only for practice."

Linda nodded. "But what should I do about spelling?"

Grampy thought a moment. "If that spelling were a basketball game and you fouled, what would happen?"

"I'd have to take a penalty," Linda answered.

"Exactly."

Linda smiled. She knew now what she had to do.

The next day at school, though, Mrs. Crandall didn't quite act like a referee. She announced that she wanted Linda and Tammy to stay after school. It was worse than a player on another team getting to shoot a free throw. Later, alone with Tammy and Mrs. Crandall after school in the classroom, was embarrassing and humiliating and extremely uncomfortable!

"I cheated," Linda blurted out.

Mrs. Crandall looked surprised. Maybe it was because she hadn't had a chance to say that the two spelling papers looked exactly alike. Both girls had missed the same three words, and they had misspelled them in exactly the same way.

"Oh? And why did you cheat, Linda?"

Linda squirmed in her seat. Maybe she should have said that she had cheated on the first spelling test and not the second, but cheating was cheating, wasn't it?

"I cheated because I wanted to get all the words right so I could be the class speller."

Now it was Tammy's turn to be surprised. For once, she didn't say anything during the whole time to Mrs. Crandall. She hadn't even had a chance to say anything against Jill. Mrs. Crandall seemed to notice that it was odd, too, as she turned to Tammy and asked, "Is that right, Tammy?"

Tammy shrugged.

"But you were the one that brought it to my attention that someone had cheated, Tammy. Don't you have anything to say?"

Tammy scratched her head. She looked up at the ceiling, then down at the floor, and then at her fingernails. Finally, she shook her head.

"Well, then, Linda, you know I will have to give you a failing grade on this spelling test." Mrs. Crandall held up the paper to indicate the last test that the class had taken. "And I'm sorry to say that I will have to give Coach Milgram a bad report about you. He's asked me to recommend you to practice with the basketball team. Now I can't do that."

Linda quaked with shock. Report to Coach Milgram about her cheating? Not play basketball?

"All right. You two are excused."

Tammy jumped up out of her seat and bounced out the door. Linda rose more slowly, shuffling along like a stunned animal. How could this have happened to her? She never thought in a million years that admitting to cheating might decide whether she would play basketball. But even more shocking was the fact that Tammy was waiting for her out in the hall.

"Why did you say that?" Tammy wanted to

know. "You didn't cheat off me. I cheated off of you!"

Linda didn't know why she had said it. She felt better after admitting that she cheated, but Mrs. Crandall didn't understand which test Linda had cheated on, and now Linda had ruined things with Coach Milgram. She shrugged.

To make things worse, there was a crowd of fourth-grade girls there, who had been waiting for Linda and Tammy to come out of the classroom.

"What happened?" Jill wanted to know.

"Mrs. Crandall isn't going to award the contest to the boys, is she?" asked Libby.

"She opened her big mouth," Tammy informed them, pointing to Linda. "She told Mrs. Crandall she cheated."

There was a big gasp from the other girls.

"But what about the party?" a girl named Sabrina Calder asked. "You said Linda's parents would put on a magic show for our class, Jill. If she said she cheated, there's no way Mrs. Crandall will let her be the class speller and win the spelling bee."

"I know for a fact that Linda didn't cheat on that test," Jill said. "We've got to find a way to change Mrs. Crandall's mind."

Jill stared at Tammy. Tammy looked away.

Linda dashed out of the school; she couldn't stay there any longer. She didn't care about the spelling anymore. But she could still see the disappointed look on Mrs. Crandall's face and hear her words about giving Coach Milgram a bad report.

Linda ran all the way to Parmalee's diner. But when she pushed at the door, it wouldn't budge. It was locked!

Linda glanced down at the sign taped on the door. In big red letters, the sign announced that Parmalee's diner was "Closed."

But where was Parmalee? Linda just had to talk to Parmalee!

She ran around to the back of the diner. She pounded and pounded on the back door until she thought her fist might split. Minutes passed. Then she heard a creaking noise and the knob turned on the door.

It was Parmalee! She was leaning on a crutch because her left leg was wrapped in a thick white cast. Parmalee had broken her leg. Now she would never be able to keep the diner! And she wouldn't be able to keep Mississippi, either. In fact, when Linda glanced around, there was no sign of the cat at all!

18

"But Bernadette," Linda pleaded, "you're the only one in the whole world who can save Parmalee!"

Bernadette looked a little like she needed saving herself. She seemed thinner than ever before, and her single candle glowing in the middle of the dining room table cast only a dim light in her house.

"Why didn't Parmalee come herself? If she needs help so badly, she should be the one asking me to take over at the diner."

Linda sighed. It wasn't easy convincing Bernadette how much Parmalee needed her. She had to think of something. She had to!

"Parmalee has a broken leg," Linda repeated. "There's no way for her to cook with a broken leg unless someone wants to wait till lunch for breakfast."

"Considering the food she cooks, I know a lot of people who would rather wait till then."

Linda couldn't deny that Parmalee was a bad cook. But she was an awfully good friend. People liked Parmalee; unlike Bernadette, they could talk easily with Parmalee. Before Parmalee broke her leg, people came into the diner and ordered her bad food just for the opportunity to spend time talking with her.

Yet, it seemed that a year of feuding between the sisters had created a barrier that Linda couldn't break through.

"But it's really our fault," Linda tried again.

"Our fault?"

This new tactic caught Bernadette's attention — just what Linda had hoped for.

Linda nodded. "Mississippi was the reason Parmalee broke her leg. She was trying to keep him from running out the door and she tripped and fell and broke her leg."

Bernadette snorted. "Parmalee never was quick on her feet. Her mouth is the thing that runs."

Linda ignored Bernadette's sour words. "But don't you see? If Mississippi hadn't been staying with Parmalee, she never would have tripped over him and broken her leg."

Bernadette's face softened, but her words were still harsh. "I'm supposed to feel guilty because your grandfather took that cat to stay with Parmalee?"

Linda shook her head. "Not guilty. You don't have to feel that. But Grampy took Mississippi to Parmalee because you couldn't spare any food to feed him. He knew you'd feed Mississippi before you fed yourself. He was trying to solve a problem for you and Mississippi."

Bernadette snorted again. "You ask me, your grandfather never had much favor for that cat in the first place. More than once I saw him shooing it out of his garage. He was more than happy to get rid of it."

Linda walked towards the door, giving up on her mission to persuade Bernadette to help Parmalee. But she couldn't help setting the record straight. "Grampy knows how much Mississippi means to *me*. And he knew my brother, Ian, was being mean to 'Sippi. He took 'Sippi to Parmalee so he wouldn't get kicked and so you wouldn't have to worry about him getting enough food."

She didn't wait for Bernadette to say anything else. Linda marched out the door and let Bernadette sit there and think about what she had said. "Simmer in her own stew," as Parmalee would have said.

And then Linda wished Bernadette could have seen what she saw: Grampy was in the garage, but he didn't hear Linda sneak up behind him. A thickness choked her chest when she saw what Grampy was doing. He was crumpling a couple of cookies into an old butter tub and placing it close to the tire where 'Sippi liked to perch. Grampy missed him, too.

At school on Friday, Mrs. Crandall handed out little pieces of paper to all the girls so they could vote on a class speller. Jill Kramer won.

Linda was happy for Jill, but she still couldn't help wondering what would have happened if she hadn't messed up her paper by spelling those three words wrong. Oh, well, that was water under the bridge, as Parmalee would have said.

"Congratulations," she said to Jill after school as they were lining up to board the buses. "You'll make a good speller Monday in the bee."

"No, I won't." Jill glanced away and then back at Linda. "Don't tell anyone else, but I'm not going to be in that bee."

"But you have to!"

"No, I don't. I'm not coming to school on Monday."

"You have to go to the dentist?"

Jill shook her head.

"You feeling sick?"

Jill shrugged. "I told you before I couldn't stand up in front of the whole school with braces."

"But they don't look that bad."

"They don't look that good, either."

"Jill! We're counting on you to be our speller. If you don't come and be our speller, it'll be like cheating."

"No, it won't. It won't be any different than you spelling those words wrong on purpose so Tammy would miss them."

Linda swallowed thickly. Jill was right — what she was doing wasn't much different than what Linda had done. But how could she make Jill understand how sorry she felt herself for not doing her best?

Linda reminded Jill of her own words. "If you don't come and be our speller, you're always going to wonder how you would have done. What if you would have won? What about that?"

Jill shrugged. "But what if everybody laughs? That could happen, too."

Linda understood why Jill was scared. She had felt the same way when her mom and dad put her in their act one time. There were so many people in the audience, and they seemed to be waiting for her to make a mistake!

"Please, Jill. Try?"

"I'll think about it." Then she ran off to catch her bus.

Linda wanted to say something more to make Jill *want* to be in the spelling bee. She sensed, though, that nothing she might say would change Jill's mind.

And then a really sinking feeling came over her: if Jill didn't come and someone else had to be chosen, she was sure it would be Tammy Collins. Tammy would think, then, that she could go on getting her way by cheating. She would be hurting herself again like Parmalee said.

But what could Linda do? She had tried, the hard way, to help Tammy, with her efforts to persuade Jill to be in the bee. There had to be a harder way. If only Linda could find it.

19

"Where's Jill? Anybody seen Jill?"

Linda searched for her friend Monday morning at school. Jill hadn't ridden the bus. Linda waited by the big double front doors, but Jill never came.

"Mrs. Crandall, Jill isn't here today," Tammy pointed out. "Who's going to be our speller in the school spelling bee?"

Mrs. Crandall stopped to think for a moment. "Does anyone know anything about Jill?"

Linda knew. She knew Jill was absent because she didn't want to be embarrassed by her braces in front of the whole school. But she didn't say anything.

While the class was doing a math assignment, Mrs. Crandall left the room to go to the office. When she came back, she announced, "Jill Kramer is sick today. Someone else will have to take her place in the spelling bee."

Linda felt sad. She was sure Jill would have been a good speller in the bee — the best speller, in fact. She was sorry that Jill was too scared to be their class speller. And she was sure Jill would eventually feel like she felt — always wondering about what might have happened if she had tried.

"Mrs. Crandall," Tammy said, raising her hand. "Can the girls vote for a new speller?"

Mrs. Crandall nodded. She passed out the little slips of paper again. "Libby, would you please pick up the votes?" she asked, after everyone was through writing and folding.

Libby stood up. She had a strange look on her face. "I . . . I . . . I can't," she muttered. "I'm sick," she managed to mumble. And then she threw up all over her desk.

Everyone in the room groaned. Libby turned white and ran from the room.

Mrs. Crandall motioned for the class to move their desks away from Libby's. "I'll go get the janitor," she promised, "and see about Libby. Meanwhile, everyone line up to go to the auditorium for the spelling bee."

"But Mrs. Crandall," Sabrina Calder called. "Who's going to be our speller?"

Mrs. Crandall quickly sorted through the thirteen pieces of paper. "Tammy Collins," she announced quickly, and then dashed out of the room.

"Oh, boy, this should be good," Eddie Wilcox said. He motioned for the other boys to huddle around him. "Let's take bets on how long Collins lasts before *she* throws up. Right there in front of the whole school!"

Sabrina nudged Tammy. "You're feeling all right, aren't you?"

Tammy shrugged. Linda didn't think Tammy looked like she felt all right. She wasn't smiling, even though she'd been chosen the speller!

Tammy glanced at Linda. The look on her face was one that Linda had never seen before: it was a look of fear.

"How are you feeling, Collins?" Ryan Soetart wanted to know, mocking Tammy by tiptoeing around her at a safe distance.

"Leave me alone, Ryan," Tammy snapped back at him.

"Think you can spell puke?"

"P-U," Eddie Wilcox began, holding his nose.

"Why don't you two leave her alone?" Linda asked, cutting between the boys and Tammy. *"You're* the ones making her sick."

"Boys and girls," Mrs. Crandall said, clapping her hands as soon as she swung into the room. "It's time now to go to the auditorium."

135

Linda fell into line behind Tammy. It seemed to her that Tammy's walk was much slower than it used to be. Her shoulders slumped, too.

Just short of the auditorium door, Tammy suddenly bolted from the line and ran to the girls' bathroom. Linda stopped and gazed after her.

"Where's Tammy?" Mrs. Crandall asked as Linda eased up to the door where the teacher was standing.

"She ran for the bathroom," Linda told her.

"Would you please go after her, Linda? I'll get the class settled and be along in a minute."

Linda slowly traced Tammy's steps to the bathroom. She pushed open the door and called into Tammy, "Are you sick?"

Tammy didn't make any noise, so Linda entered the room and looked for her. She was leaning into a corner, looking down at the floor.

"Are you sick?" Linda repeated.

Tammy shrugged.

"You're scared you might get sick, aren't you?" Linda asked.

"It happened to Jill and Libby," Tammy muttered.

Linda sighed. She could understand how Tammy felt, since the boys had teased her so badly. But something Grampy once said stuck in her brain. "All that back there was just talk from those boys. So you'd lose your head."

"You think you're so smart," Tammy said hatefully, "because you have magicians for parents. I suppose now you're going to trick Mrs. Crandall into picking you to be the class speller."

Linda shook her head. "I'm going to stay here with you. Somebody else can be the class speller."

A look of surprise lit Tammy's face. "Don't you want to be the class speller?"

Linda shrugged. "I only wanted to be the speller so other kids would like me. But you know what? Jill started liking me . . . really liking me, when she found out how much we were the same instead of how much we were different."

"Well, there's nothing the same about you and me," Tammy sniffed.

Linda thought about that for a moment. What *did* she and Tammy have in common?

"There has to be *something,*" Linda said thoughtfully.

"We don't look anything alike," Tammy pointed out. "And I don't have magician parents like you do."

"No," Linda agreed, "but maybe sometimes we feel the same."

Tammy frowned. "What do you mean?"

"I mean like right now you're feeling too scared to be in the spelling bee."

"I am not!"

"Doesn't your stomach feel like the floor dropped out from under you?"

Tammy scowled.

"Isn't your heart beating like a bongo drum?"

Tammy shrugged.

"That was the way I felt the first day I came to school here."

"You did?"

Linda nodded.

Tammy glanced down at the ground. "Yeah, I guess that's how I feel right now. I guess maybe there *is* something about us that's the same."

Linda smiled. "Well, I hope you don't do what I did."

"What?"

"I was so scared that I cheated on that first spelling test."

"I know," Tammy mumbled. "But it was easy for you to cheat on a spelling test. I can't go in there and be something I'm not!"

"Just tell Mrs. Crandall you don't want to be in the spelling bee."

"And get called a scaredy cat by everybody?"

"There are worse things than being a scaredy cat. You could be a scaredy cat with no friends. But you're not, because I'm your friend."

Tammy couldn't say anything for a moment. Finally she said, "I think there's something else about us that's the same."

"What?"

"I can spell Mississippi," Tammy said proudly. "And you have a cat that can spell Mississippi."

Linda smiled. "I think there's something else that's the same about us."

"What?"

"I don't think either one of us is ever going to cheat again."

Tammy smiled.

20

When Linda and Tammy returned to the entrance of the auditorium, Mrs. Crandall had just stepped out into the hall in search of them.

Linda glanced at Tammy. It was a look that told her friend she was there beside her, that Tammy was not alone.

"I don't want to be in the spelling bee, Mrs. Crandall," Tammy told their teacher.

"Are you sick?" Mrs. Crandall asked.

Tammy shook her head. "I just don't want to be the speller."

Mrs. Crandall looked confused, but she didn't ask why Tammy didn't want to be the speller. She ushered the two of them to their seats with the rest of the class, and then she said to Sabrina Calder, "Would you like to be our class speller?"

Sabrina's eyes lit up. She nodded her head. Mrs. Crandall motioned for Sabrina to leave her seat and take her place on the stage up front with the other spellers.

"What's the matter with Collins?" Eddie Wilcox wanted to know. "She chicken out?"

The rest of the class whispered and pointed at Tammy. Linda seated herself like a barrier between Tammy and the others. "Tammy doesn't have to be the speller if she doesn't want to."

"Yeah, she's a scaredy cat all right," Eddie Wilcox decided.

"Takes one to know one," Linda said to Eddie.

"Guess that makes you a scaredy cat, too," Eddie said to Linda.

"I guess it does," Linda said with satisfaction, smiling at Tammy. "But sometimes being scared can make you find out who you are. Tammy's good at organizing things, and I'm good at playing basketball."

Eddie was so surprised that Linda had agreed with him that he shut up!

The attention of the class shifted to the stage, where eight spellers drew numbers from a box and rearranged themselves in the order of their numbers. Number one was a girl from the sixth grade. She wore glasses *and* braces. Linda wished Jill was there to see that girl.

Second was a little third-grade boy who dipped in height next to a fifth-grade girl. Sabrina Calder had drawn number four, so she stood next, and following her were another third-grader, Ian, a fourth-grade boy from another class, and a fifth-grade girl. Linda didn't know any of the students except Sabrina and Ian. But which of the two of them should she root for?

Her decision was easy when she saw Grampy and Grams enter the auditorium at the back. Grampy waved his little finger at her — their special sign.

Finally, the bee began. All the spellers sat down in chairs until it was their turn to try spelling a word. The fifth-grade girl spelled the first word without even stopping to think about it. Down the line, all eight of them spelled easy words. But by round two, the words were getting harder.

"Marshmallow," Mrs. Duncan, the speech teacher, enunciated.

It was the third-grader's turn. He stood up and rubbed his chin. "Marshmallow. M-A-R-C-H ..."

Mrs. Duncan frowned and motioned for the boy to go sit down in the auditorium.

The fifth-grade girl next to Sabrina stood up. Her word was "acceptance." "A-C-E-P ..."

Mrs. Duncan frowned again. The fifth-grade girl snapped her fingers in disgust and exited the stage.

It was Sabrina's turn. She rose slowly. "Exaggerate." "E-X-A-G-G-E-R-A-T-E."

Mrs. Duncan smiled. Linda's class clapped and hooted at Sabrina's perfect spelling.

Next, a third-grader spelled his word. Then it was Ian's turn. He spelled his word easily. Linda clapped. The solitary clap made everybody surrounding Linda turn and look at her, but she went right on clapping. She knew something they didn't: she knew that everybody needed somebody to cheer them on. And she knew now that supporting somebody else's efforts was just as important as being the star yourself.

"How come you're clapping?" Tammy asked her.

"I promised my brother I'd clap for him."

"But everybody in our class is going to think you're a traitor," Tammy said.

"Well, they'll just have to think that," Linda said. "I know I'm not a traitor. That's what's important. And if *they* had a brother in the bee, they'd probably do the same thing."

Next, the fourth-grader next to Ian stumbled on

the word "macaroni." He spelled it with two c's. Then the fifth-grader on the end spelled "apparent" with two r's. Both were out of the bee. That left only four spellers: the sixth-grade girl, Sabrina, a third-grade girl, and Ian.

Two more rounds of words went by with none of the four stumbling on them.

In the next round, Mrs. Duncan finally pronounced a word that the sixth-grade girl next to Sabrina couldn't spell. It was "hygiene." Dejectedly, she left the stage.

Sabrina heaved a deep breath and then spelled her word. "C-O-N-F-I-D-E-N-C-E."

Mrs. Duncan nodded. Sabrina went back to her seat with a big applause from Linda's fourth grade.

The third-grade girl spelled "giraffe." With only three spellers left, it was Ian's turn. His word was "accidental." He spelled it easily, and Linda clapped again, amid a sea of stares.

Now it was back to Sabrina again. She spelled "temperature." Her fourth-grade class whooped when she got it right. Linda whooped right along with them.

Next came the word "ability." The third-grade girl misspelled it. But Ian spelled "spaghetti" correctly.

Linda's solitary clap and Grams and Grampy's claps from the back of the auditorium sounded thin and hollow. But Ian smiled, and Linda knew he appreciated it.

There were only two of them left! Ian and Sabrina!

Now it was Sabrina's turn. Her word was "description." Slowly, she sounded out the syllables and spelled the word correctly.

They went through three more rounds that way. Ian spelled his word. And then Sabrina spelled hers. Mrs. Duncan searched for harder words.

Sabrina spelled "cough." Ian spelled "antenna."

Sabrina spelled "reasonable." Ian spelled "circumference."

Sabrina spelled "fascinating." Ian spelled "quirk."

Round after round they went, each spelling their words, until Sabrina slipped on the word "colleague." She forgot one of the l's.

Mrs. Duncan raised her hand to the audience to indicate that they should remain seated. "Since I gave a word to Sabrina, I must give one to Ian, and he must spell that word plus another correctly before I can declare a winner."

Everybody sat back down in their seats. Mrs. Duncan faced Ian. "Auxiliary," she said.

Ian coughed. He squinted. But letter by letter, he spelled the word. Then he spelled "khaki." He was the new Riverview Elementary Spelling Champion!

21

Linda jumped out of her seat and bounded up the auditorium aisle, quickly scaling the steps onto the stage. She thought she might bust with excitement! Ian had won! Ian had won!

"Ian, you did it!" she yelled, grabbing him around the neck.

Ian smiled. He clasped hands with a throng of kids who had followed Linda up onto the stage to congratulate him. They might not have clapped for Ian during the bee, but now they could see Ian for who he really was. And the broad smile on Ian's face proved to Linda that Ian had discovered himself!

"Any chance your parents might put on a magic show for the whole school while they're in town?" Cory Richards asked.

"You can count on it," Ian said. And they actually shook hands!

Coach Milgram was also one of those congratulating Ian. "The Spelling Cappanelli," he called Ian, smiling and shaking his hand. Then he turned to Linda. "Thought about basketball practice, Linda?"

Linda shrugged. She was surprised that after a bad report from Mrs. Crandall, Coach Milgram still wanted her to join basketball practice. "You still want me to practice?"

Coach Milgram nodded. "Everybody makes mistakes," he said. "The trick is to learn from them."

"Gosh, yes!" Linda exclaimed. "I want to play more than anything! I'll be at the next practice."

Coach Milgram smiled and nodded. He was going to give Linda a second chance!

Then Mrs. Duncan handed Ian his medal. He rubbed at it with his finger, as if to prove it was really there, that he had really won it.

"My, we're so proud of you, Ian," Grams said. "This is just wonderful. I knew you could do it. After all, champion spellers run in the family." Her face beamed and she seemed to stand taller, as if she'd won the medal herself.

"Don't puff up too much, old woman," Grampy said. "Or you're liable to pop. Besides, Ian won that medal on his own. With no help from anybody."

Ian glanced down. "Well, maybe that's not completely true. I think I did have some help. I think somebody showed me how to find out about myself."

"What do you mean?" Grampy asked.

"This lady called yesterday. It was about your cat, Linda."

Linda gasped, "Mississippi!"

"Yeah. She asked if Linda was home, and when I said she'd gone to the store with Grams and Grampy, she asked me to come and catch the cat right away. It had come back from running off. But she couldn't catch it because her leg was in a cast. She said her sister couldn't catch it either. She was too busy cooking or something."

"That was Parmalee!" Linda exclaimed. "Mississippi came back to Parmalee's! And Bernadette and Parmalee made up! Bernadette is cooking at the diner!"

"Well, I'll be fit to be tied," Grampy said. "Sure sounds like it."

"Did you go catch Mississippi, Ian?" Linda asked excitedly.

"I didn't want to. I told the lady that. But she

told me she'd give me something good to eat for doing it. So I went."

"Did you catch Mississippi?" Linda jumped up and down in anticipation.

"That cat is half wild! Soon as I would get close, *wham*! Off he'd go, just beyond my reach. Finally, I got so fed up I told the lady I was going to quit! So she gave me the pie she promised, and I was just about to leave when something funny happened."

"What?" Linda said.

Ian glanced down, hesitatant about telling the rest of the story. When he looked up, he said, "It sounded to me like that cat was spelling."

Linda looked at Grampy. Grampy winked at her.

"All the way home, I got to thinking about that cat," Ian confided. "I got to thinking about what it could mean that that cat could spell. And I got to thinking about how that lady didn't even seem upset that I never did catch the cat. It was like she'd called me there to hear the cat spell instead."

Linda's eyes lit up. "She was acting like a go-between!"

"A what?" Ian asked.

"A spelling cat?" Grams asked skeptically. "I've never heard of such a thing."

"I have," Linda assured her grandmother. "And so has Grampy."

Grampy nodded at Grams. But Grams still didn't believe it.

"Well, it may sound funny," Ian said, "but that's why I think I did so well in the spelling bee. Trying to catch that cat made me realize the spelling bee wasn't dumb after all. It was just as important as basketball."

"That I can understand," Grams said.

"What else did you learn, Ian?" Linda wanted to know.

Ian shrugged. "Well, I learned that I'm an awful lot like that cat. I don't let anybody get close to me. That's why I don't have any friends. I'm good at spelling, but being good at something doesn't get a person a friend. To get a friend, you've got to be a friend." Ian handed his medal to Grams. "Keep that for me?"

Grams nodded. "But where are you going?"

Ian smiled. "Linda and I are going to the 'Friends Again Diner.' With both of us trying, this time I'm sure we can catch Mississippi and bring him home."

Linda smiled. So Parmalee and Bernadette *had* really made up, so much so that they even changed the name of the diner! "Friends Again" was the best name they could have picked, Linda decided. She couldn't wait to tell them both so!

She and Ian took off running. Bounding off the stage. Loping up the auditorium aisle. Matching each other, stride for stride. There wasn't anything they couldn't do. Together.